GU00992989

Jacob Abbott

Cleopatra

Jacob Abbott

Cleopatra

1st Edition | ISBN: 978-3-73406-691-7

Place of Publication: Frankfurt am Main, Germany

Year of Publication: 2019

Outlook Verlag GmbH, Germany.

Reproduction of the original.

CLEOPATRA

BY

JACOB ABBOTT

PREFACE

Of all the beautiful women of history, none has left us such convincing proofs of her charms as Cleopatra, for the tide of Rome's destiny, and, therefore, that of the world, turned aside because of her beauty. Julius Caesar, whose legions trampled the conquered world from Canopus to the Thames, capitulated to her, and Mark Antony threw a fleet, an empire and his own honor to the winds to follow her to his destruction. Disarmed at last before the frigid Octavius, she found her peerless body measured by the cold eye of her captor only for the triumphal procession, and the friendly asp alone spared her Rome's crowning ignominy.

TABLE OF CONTENTS

ILLUSTRATIONS

CLEOPATRA

MEETING OF CLEOPATRA AND ANTONY

CLEOPATRA TESTING THE POISON UPON THE SLAVES

CHAPTER I.

The parentage and birth of Cleopatra.—Cleopatra's residence in Egypt.—Physical aspect of Egypt.—The eagle's wings and science.—Physical peculiarities of Egypt connected with the laws of rain.—General laws of rain.—Causes which modify the quantity of rain.—Striking contrasts.—Rainless regions.—Great rainless region of Asia and Africa.—The Andes.—Map of the rainless region.—Valley of the Nile.—The Red Sea.—The oases.—Siweh.—Mountains of the Moon.—The River Nile.—Incessant rains.—Inundation of the Nile.—Course of the river.—Subsidence of the waters.—Luxuriant vegetation.—Absence of forests.—Great antiquity of Egypt.—Her monuments.—The Delta of the Nile.—The Delta as seen from the sea.—Pelusiac mouth of the Nile.—The Canopic mouth.—Ancient Egypt.—The Pyramids.—Conquests of the Persians and Macedonians.—The Ptolemies.—Founding of Alexandria.—The Pharos.

The story of Cleopatra is a story of crime. It is a narrative of the course and the consequences of unlawful love. In her strange and romantic history we see this passion portrayed with the most complete and graphic fidelity in all its influences and effects; its uncontrollable impulses, its intoxicating joys, its reckless and mad career, and the dreadful remorse and ultimate despair and ruin in which it always and inevitably ends.

Cleopatra was by birth an Egyptian; by ancestry and descent she was a Greek. Thus, while Alexandria and the Delta of the Nile formed the scene of the most important events and incidents of her history, it was the blood of Macedon which flowed in her veins. Her character and action are marked by the genius, the courage, the originality, and the impulsiveness pertaining to the stock from which she sprung. The events of her history, on the other hand, and the peculiar character of her adventures, her sufferings, and her sins, were determined by the circumstances with which she was surrounded, and the influences which were brought to bear upon her in the soft and voluptuous clime where the scenes of her early life were laid.

Egypt has always been considered as physically the most remarkable country on the globe. It is a long and narrow valley of verdure and fruitfulness, completely insulated from the rest of the habitable world. It is more completely insulated, in fact, than any literal island could be, inasmuch as deserts are more impassable than seas. The very existence of Egypt is a most extraordinary phenomenon. If we could but soar with the wings of an eagle

4

into the air, and look down upon the scene, so as to observe the operation of that grand and yet simple process by which this long and wonderful valley, teeming so profusely with animal and vegetable life, has been formed, and is annually revivified and renewed, in the midst of surrounding wastes of silence, desolation, and death, we should gaze upon it with never-ceasing admiration and pleasure. We have not the wings of the eagle, but the generalizations of science furnish us with a sort of substitute for them.

The long series of patient, careful, and sagacious observations, which have been continued now for two thousand years, bring us results, by means of which, through our powers of mental conception, we may take a comprehensive survey of the whole scene, analogous, in some respects, to that which direct and actual vision would afford us, if we could look down upon it from the eagle's point of view. It is, however, somewhat humiliating to our pride of intellect to reflect that long-continued philosophical investigations and learned scientific research are, in such a case as this, after all, in some sense, only a sort of substitute for wings. A human mind connected with a pair of eagle's wings would have solved the mystery of Egypt in a week; whereas science, philosophy, and research, confined to the surface of the ground, have been occupied for twenty centuries in accomplishing the undertaking.

It is found at last that both the existence of Egypt itself, and its strange insulation in the midst of boundless tracts of dry and barren sand, depend upon certain remarkable results of the general laws of rain. The water which is taken up by the atmosphere from the surface of the sea and of the land by evaporation, falls again, under certain circumstances, in showers of rain, the frequency and copiousness of which vary very much in different portions of the earth. As a general principle, rains are much more frequent and abundant near the equator than in temperate climes, and they grow less and less so as we approach the poles. This might naturally have been expected; for, under the burning sun of the equator, the evaporation of water must necessarily go on with immensely greater rapidity than in the colder zones, and all the water which is taken up must, of course, again come down.

It is not, however, wholly by the latitude of the region in which the evaporation takes place that the quantity of rain which falls from the atmosphere is determined; for the condition on which the falling back, in rain, of the water which has been taken up by evaporation mainly depends, is the cooling of the atmospheric stratum which contains it; and this effect is produced in very various ways, and many different causes operate to modify it. Sometimes the stratum is cooled by being wafted over ranges of mountains, sometimes by encountering and becoming mingled with cooler currents of air; and sometimes, again, by being driven in winds toward a higher, and, consequently, cooler latitude. If, on the other hand, air moves from cold mountains toward warm and sunny plains, or from higher latitudes to lower, or if, among the various currents into which it falls, it becomes mixed with air warmer than itself, its capacity for containing vapor in solution is increased, and, consequently, instead of releasing its hold upon the waters which it has already in possession, it becomes thirsty for more. It moves over a country, under these circumstances, as a warm and drying wind. Under a reverse of circumstances it would have formed drifting mists, or, perhaps, even copious showers of rain.

It will be evident, from these considerations, that the frequency of the showers, and the quantity of the rain which will fall, in the various regions respectively which the surface of the earth presents, must depend on the combined influence of many causes, such as the warmth of the climate, the proximity and the direction of mountains and of seas, the character of the prevailing winds, and the reflecting qualities of the soil. These and other similar causes, it is found, do, in fact, produce a vast difference in the quantity of rain which falls in different regions. In the northern part of South America, where the land is bordered on every hand by vast tropical seas, which load the hot and thirsty air with vapor, and where the mighty Cordillera of the Andes rears its icy summits to chill and precipitate the vapors again, a quantity of rain amounting to more than ten feet in perpendicular height falls in a year. At St. Petersburg, on the other hand, the quantity thus falling in a year is but little more than one foot. The immense deluge which pours down from the clouds in South America would, if the water were to remain where it fell, wholly submerge and inundate the country. As it is, in flowing off through the valleys to the sea, the united torrents form the greatest river on the globe—the Amazon; and the vegetation, stimulated by the heat, and nourished by the abundant and incessant supplies of moisture, becomes so rank, and loads the earth with such an entangled and matted mass of trunks, and stems, and twining wreaths and vines, that man is almost excluded from the scene. The boundless forests become a vast and almost impenetrable jungle, abandoned to wild beasts, noxious reptiles, and huge and ferocious birds of prey.

Of course, the district of St. Petersburg, with its icy winter, its low and powerless sun, and its twelve inches of annual rain, must necessarily present, in all its phenomena of vegetable and animal life, a striking contrast to the exuberant prolificness of New Grenada. It is, however, after all, not absolutely the opposite extreme. There are certain regions on the surface of the earth that are actually rainless; and it is these which present us with the true and real contrast to the luxuriant vegetation and teeming life of the country of the Amazon. In these rainless regions all is necessarily silence, desolation, and death. No plant can grow; no animal can live. Man, too, is forever and hopelessly excluded. If the exuberant abundance of animal and vegetable life shut him out, in some measure, from regions which an excess of heat and moisture render too prolific, the total absence of them still more effectually forbids him a home in these. They become, therefore, vast wastes of dry and barren sands in which no root can find nourishment, and of dreary rocks to which not even a lichen can cling.

The most extensive and remarkable rainless region on the earth is a vast tract extending through the interior and northern part of Africa, and the southwestern part of Asia. The Red Sea penetrates into this tract from the south, and thus breaks the outline and continuity of its form, without, however, altering, or essentially modifying its character. It divides it, however, and to the different portions which this division forms, different names have been given. The Asiatic portion is called Arabia Deserta; the African tract has received the name of Sahara; while between these two, in the neighborhood of Egypt, the barren region is called simply *the desert*. The whole tract is marked, however, throughout, with one all-pervading character: the absence of vegetable, and, consequently, of animal life, on account of the absence of rain. The rising of a range of lofty mountains in the center of it, to produce a precipitation of moisture from the air, would probably transform the whole of the vast waste into as verdant, and fertile, and populous a region as any on the globe.

[Illustration: VALLEY OF THE NILE]

As it is, there are no such mountains. The whole tract is nearly level, and so little elevated above the sea, that, at the distance of many hundred miles in the interior, the land rises only to the height of a few hundred feet above the surface of the Mediterranean; whereas in New Grenada, at less than one hundred miles from the sea, the chain of the Andes rises to elevations of from ten to fifteen thousand feet. Such an ascent as that of a few hundred feet in hundreds of miles would be wholly imperceptible to any ordinary mode of observation; and the great rainless region, accordingly, of Africa and Asia is, as it appears to the traveler, one vast plain, a thousand miles wide and five thousand miles long, with only one considerable interruption to the dead monotony which reigns, with that exception, every where over the immense expanse of silence and solitude. The single interval of fruitfulness and life is the valley of the Nile.

There are, however, in fact, three interruptions to the continuity of this plain, though only one of them constitutes any considerable interruption to its barrenness. They are all of them valleys, extending from north to south, and lying side by side. The most easterly of these valleys is so deep that the waters of the ocean flow into it from the south, forming a long and narrow inlet called the Red Sea. As this inlet communicates freely with the ocean, it is always nearly of the same level, and as the evaporation from it is not sufficient to produce rain, it does not even fertilize its own shores. Its presence varies the dreary scenery of the landscape, it is true, by giving us surging waters to look upon instead of driving sands; but this is all. With the exception of the spectacle of an English steamer passing, at weary intervals, over its dreary expanse, and some moldering remains of ancient cities on its eastern shore, it affords scarcely any indications of life. It does very little, therefore, to relieve the monotonous aspect of solitude and desolation which reigns over the region into which it has intruded.

The most westerly of the three valleys to which we have alluded is only a slight depression of the surface of the land marked by a line of *oases*. The depression is not sufficient to admit the waters of the Mediterranean, nor are there any rains over any portion of the valley which it forms sufficient to make it the bed of a stream. Springs issue, however, here and there, in several places, from the ground, and, percolating through the sands along the valley, give fertility to little dells, long and narrow, which, by the contrast that they form with the surrounding desolation, seem to the traveler to possess the verdure and beauty of Paradise. There is a line of these oases extending along this westerly depression, and some of them are of considerable extent. The oasis of Siweh, on which stood the far-famed temple of Jupiter Ammon, was many miles in extent, and was said to have contained in ancient times a population of eight thousand souls. Thus, while the most easterly of the three valleys which we have named was sunk so low as to admit the ocean to flow freely into it, the most westerly was so slightly depressed that it gained only a circumscribed and limited fertility through the springs, which, in the lowest portions of it, oozed from the ground. The third valley—the central one—remains now to be described.

The reader will observe, by referring once more to the map, that south of the great rainless region of which we are speaking, there lie groups and ranges of mountains in Abyssinia, called the Mountains of the Moon. These mountains are near the equator, and the relation which they sustain to the surrounding seas, and to currents of wind which blow in that quarter of the world, is such, that they bring down from the atmosphere, especially in certain seasons of the year, vast and continual torrents of rain. The water which thus falls drenches the mountain sides and deluges the valleys. There is a great portion of it which can not flow to the southward or eastward toward the sea, as the whole country consists, in those directions, of continuous tracts of elevated land. The rush of water thus turns to the northward, and, pressing on across the desert through the great central valley which we have referred to above, it finds an outlet, at last, in the Mediterranean, at a point two thousand miles distant from the place where the immense condenser drew it from the skies. The river thus created is the Nile. It is formed, in a word, by the surplus waters of a district inundated with rains, in their progress across a rainless desert, seeking the sea.

If the surplus of water upon the Abyssinian mountains had been constant and uniform, the stream, in its passage across the desert, would have communicated very little fertility to the barren sands which it traversed. The immediate banks of the river would have, perhaps, been fringed with verdure, but the influence of the irrigation would have extended no farther than the water itself could have reached, by percolation through the sand. But the flow of the water is not thus uniform and steady. In a certain season of the year the rains are incessant, and they descend with such abundance and profusion as almost to inundate the districts where they fall. Immense torrents stream down the mountain sides; the valleys are deluged; plains turn into morasses, and morasses into lakes. In a word, the country becomes half submerged, and the accumulated mass of waters would rush with great force and violence down the central valley of the desert, which forms their only outlet, if the passage were narrow, and if it made any considerable descent in its course to the sea. It is, however, not narrow, and the descent is very small. The depression in the surface of the desert, through which the water flows, is from five to ten miles wide, and, though it is nearly two thousand miles from the rainy district across the desert to the sea, the country for the whole distance is almost level. There is only sufficient descent, especially for the last thousand miles, to determine a very gentle current to the northward in the waters of the stream.

Under these circumstances, the immense quantity of water which falls in the rainy district in these inundating tropical showers, expands over the whole valley, and forms for a time an immense lake, extending in length across the whole breadth of the desert. This lake is, of course, from five to ten miles wide, and a thousand miles long. The water in it is shallow and turbid, and it has a gentle current toward the north. The rains, at length, in a great measure cease; but it requires some months for the water to run off and leave the valley dry. As soon as it is gone, there springs up from the whole surface of the ground which has been thus submerged a most rank and luxuriant vegetation.

This vegetation, now wholly regulated and controlled by the hand of man, must have been, in its original and primeval state, of a very peculiar character. It must have consisted of such plants only as could exist under the condition of having the soil in which they grew laid, for a quarter of the year, wholly under water. This circumstance, probably, prevented the valley of the Nile from having been, like other fertile tracts of land, encumbered, in its native state, with forests. For the same reason, wild beasts could never have haunted it. There were no forests to shelter them, and no refuge or retreat for them but the dry and barren desert, during the period of the annual inundations. This most extraordinary valley seems thus to have been formed and preserved by Nature herself for the special possession of man. She herself seems to have held it in reserve for him from the very morning of creation, refusing admission into it to every plant and every animal that might hinder or disturb his occupancy and control. And if he were to abandon it now for a thousand years, and then return to it once more, he would find it just as he left it, ready for his immediate possession. There would be no wild beasts that he must first expel, and no tangled forests would have sprung up, that his ax must first remove. Nature is the husbandman who keeps this garden of the world in order, and the means and machinery by which she operates are the grand evaporating surfaces of the seas, the beams of the tropical sun, the lofty summits of the Abyssinian Mountains, and, as the product and result of all this instrumentality, great periodical inundations of summer rain.

For these or some other reasons Egypt has been occupied by man from the most remote antiquity. The oldest records of the human race, made three thousand years ago, speak of Egypt as ancient then, when they were written. Not only is Tradition silent, but even Fable herself does not attempt to tell the story of the origin of her population. Here stand the oldest and most enduring monuments that human power has ever been able to raise. It is, however, somewhat humiliating to the pride of the race to reflect that the loftiest and proudest, as well as the most permanent and stable of all the works which man has ever accomplished, are but the incidents and adjuncts of a thin stratum of alluvial fertility, left upon the sands by the subsiding waters of summer showers.

The most important portion of the alluvion of the Nile is the northern portion, where the valley widens and opens toward the sea, forming a triangular plain of about one hundred miles in length on each of the sides, over which the waters of the river flow in a great number of separate creeks and channels. The whole area forms a vast meadow, intersected every where with slow-flowing streams of water, and presenting on its surface the most enchanting pictures of fertility, abundance, and beauty. This region is called the Delta of the Nile.

The sea upon the coast is shallow, and the fertile country formed by the deposits of the river seems to have projected somewhat beyond the line of the coast; although, as the land has not advanced perceptibly for the last eighteen hundred years, it may be somewhat doubtful whether the whole of the apparent protrusion is not due to the natural conformation of the coast, rather than to any changes made by the action of the river.

The Delta of the Nile is so level itself, and so little raised above the level of the Mediterranean, that the land seems almost a continuation of the same surface with the sea, only, instead of blue waters topped with white-crested waves, we have broad tracts of waving grain, and gentle swells of land crowned with hamlets and villages. In approaching the coast, the navigator has no distant view of all this verdure and beauty. It lies so low that it continues beneath the horizon until the ship is close upon the shore. The first landmarks, in fact, which the seaman makes, are the tops of trees growing apparently out of the water, or the summit of an obelisk, or the capital of a pillar, marking the site of some ancient and dilapidated city.

The most easterly of the channels by which the waters of the river find their way through the Delta to the sea, is called, as it will be seen marked upon the map, the Pelusiac branch. It forms almost the boundary of the fertile region of the Delta on the eastern side. There was an ancient city named Pelusium near the mouth of it. This was, of course, the first Egyptian city reached by those who arrived by land from the eastward, traveling along the shores of the Mediterranean Sea. On account of its thus marking the eastern frontier of the country, it became a point of great importance, and is often mentioned in the histories of ancient times.

The westernmost mouth of the Nile, on the other hand, was called the Canopic mouth. The distance along the coast from the Canopic mouth to Pelusium was about a hundred miles. The outline of the coast was formerly, as it still continues to be, very irregular, and the water shallow. Extended banks of sand protruded into the sea, and the sea itself, as if in retaliation, formed innumerable creeks, and inlets, and lagoons in the land. Along this irregular and uncertain boundary the waters of the Nile and the surges of the Mediterranean kept up an eternal war, with energies so nearly equal, that now, after the lapse of eighteen hundred years since the state of the contest began to be recorded, neither side has been found to have gained any perceptible advantage over the other. The river brings the sands down, and the sea drives them incessantly back, keeping the whole line of the shore in such a condition as to make it extremely dangerous and difficult of access to man.

It will be obvious, from this description of the valley of the Nile, that it formed a country which was in ancient times isolated and secluded, in a very striking manner, from all the rest of the world. It was wholly shut in by deserts, on every side, by land; and the shoals, and sand-bars, and other dangers of navigation which marked the line of the coast, seemed to forbid approach by sea. Here it remained for many ages, under the rule of its own native ancient kings. Its population was peaceful and industrious. Its scholars were famed throughout the world for their learning, their science, and their philosophy.

It was in these ages, before other nations had intruded upon its peaceful seclusion, that the Pyramids were built, and the enormous monoliths carved, and those vast temples reared whose ruined columns are now the wonder of mankind. During these remote ages, too, Egypt was, as now, the land of perpetual fertility and abundance. There would always be corn in Egypt, wherever else famine might rage. The neighboring nations and tribes in Arabia, Palestine, and Syria, found their way to it, accordingly, across the deserts on the eastern side, when driven by want, and thus opened a way of communication. At length the Persian monarchs, after extending their empire westward to the Mediterranean, found access by the same road to Pelusium, and thence overran and conquered the country. At last, about two hundred and fifty years before the time of Cleopatra, Alexander the Great, when he subverted the Persian empire, took possession of Egypt, and annexed it, among the other Persian provinces, to his own dominions. At the division of Alexander's empire, after his death, Egypt fell to one of his generals, named Ptolemy. Ptolemy made it his kingdom, and left it, at his death, to his heirs. A long line of sovereigns succeeded him, known in history as the dynasty of the Ptolemies—Greek princes, reigning over an Egyptian realm. Cleopatra was the daughter of the eleventh in the line.

The capital of the Ptolemies was Alexandria. Until the time of Alexander's conquest, Egypt had no sea-port. There were several landing-places along the coast, but no proper harbor. In fact Egypt had then so little commercial intercourse with the rest of the world, that she scarcely needed any. Alexander's engineers, however, in exploring the shore, found a point not far from the Canopic mouth of the Nile where the water was deep, and where there was an anchorage ground protected by an island. Alexander founded a city there, which he called by his own name. He perfected the harbor by artificial excavations and embankments. A lofty light-house was reared, which formed a landmark by day, and exhibited a blazing star by night to guide the galleys of the Mediterranean in. A canal was made to connect the port with the Nile, and warehouses were erected to contain the stores of merchandise. In a word, Alexandria became at once a great commercial capital. It was the seat, for several centuries, of the magnificent government of the Ptolemies; and so well was its situation chosen for the purposes intended, that it still continues, after the lapse of twenty centuries of revolution and change, one of the principal emporiums of the commerce of the East.

CHAPTER II.

The founder of the dynasty of the Ptolemies—the ruler into whose hands the
kingdom of Egypt fell, as has already been stated, at the death of Alexander
the Great—was a Macedonian general in Alexander's army. The
circumstances of his birth, and the events which led to his entering into the
service of Alexander, were somewhat peculiar. His mother, whose name was
Arsinoe, was a personal favorite and companion of Philip, king of Macedon,
the father of Alexander. Philip at length gave Arsinoe in marriage to a certain
man of his court named Lagus. A very short time after the marriage, Ptolemy
was born. Philip treated the child with the same consideration and favor that
he had evinced toward the mother. The boy was called the son of Lagus, but
his position in the royal court of Macedon was as high and honorable, and the
attentions which he received were as great, as he could have expected to
enjoy if he had been in reality a son of the king. As he grew up, he attained to
official stations of considerable responsibility and power.

In the course of time, a certain transaction occurred by means of which
Ptolemy involved himself in serious difficulty with Philip, though by the
same means he made Alexander very strongly his friend. There was a
province of the Persian empire called Caria, situated in the southwestern part
of Asia Minor. The governor of this province had offered his daughter to
Philip as the wife of one of his sons named Aridaeus, the half brother of
Alexander. Alexander's mother, who was not the mother of Aridaeus, was

jealous of this proposed marriage. She thought that it was part of a scheme for bringing Aridaeus forward into public notice, and finally making him the heir to Philip's throne; whereas she was very earnest that this splendid inheritance should be reserved for her own son. Accordingly, she proposed to Alexander that they should send a secret embassage to the Persian governor, and represent to him that it would be much better, both for him and for his daughter, that she should have Alexander instead of Aridaeus for a husband, and induce him, if possible, to demand of Philip that he should make the change.

Alexander entered readily into this scheme, and various courtiers, Ptolemy among the rest, undertook to aid him in the accomplishment of it. The embassy was sent. The governor of Caria was very much pleased with the change which they proposed to him. In fact, the whole plan seemed to be going on very successfully toward its accomplishment, when, by some means or other, Philip discovered the intrigue. He went immediately into Alexander's apartment, highly excited with resentment and anger. He had never intended to make Aridaeus, whose birth on the mother's side was obscure and ignoble, the heir to his throne, and he reproached Alexander in the bitterest terms for being of so debased and degenerate a spirit as to desire to marry the daughter of a Persian governor; a man who was, in fact, the mere slave, as he said, of a barbarian king.

Alexander's scheme was thus totally defeated; and so displeased was his father with the officers who had undertaken to aid him in the execution of it, that he banished them all from the kingdom. Ptolemy, in consequence of this decree, wandered about an exile from his country for some years, until at length the death of Philip enabled Alexander to recall him. Alexander succeeded his father as King of Macedon, and immediately made Ptolemy one of his principal generals. Ptolemy rose, in fact, to a very high command in the Macedonian army, and distinguished himself very greatly in all the celebrated conqueror's subsequent campaigns. In the Persian invasion, Ptolemy commanded one of the three grand divisions of the army, and he rendered repeatedly the most signal services to the cause of his master. He was employed on the most distant and dangerous enterprises, and was often intrusted with the management of affairs of the utmost importance. He was very successful in all his undertakings. He conquered armies, reduced fortresses, negotiated treaties, and evinced, in a word, the highest degree of military energy and skill. He once saved Alexander's life by discovering and revealing a dangerous conspiracy which had been formed against the king. Alexander had the opportunity to requite this favor, through a divine interposition vouchsafed to him, it was said, for the express purpose of enabling him to evince his gratitude. Ptolemy had been wounded by a poisoned arrow, and when all the remedies and antidotes of the physicians had failed, and the patient was apparently about to die, an effectual means of cure was revealed to Alexander in a dream, and Ptolemy, in his turn, was saved.

At the great rejoicings at Susa, when Alexander's conquests were completed, Ptolemy was honored with a golden crown, and he was married, with great pomp and ceremony, to Artacama, the daughter of one of the most distinguished Persian generals.

At length Alexander died suddenly, after a night of drinking and carousal at Babylon. He had no son old enough to succeed him, and his immense empire was divided among his generals. Ptolemy obtained Egypt for his share. He repaired immediately to Alexandria, with a great army, and a great number of Greek attendants and followers, and there commenced a reign which continued, in great prosperity and splendor, for forty years. The native Egyptians were reduced, of course, to subjection and bondage. All the offices in the army, and all stations of trust and responsibility in civil life, were filled by Greeks. Alexandria was a Greek city, and it became at once one of the most important commercial centers in all those seas. Greek and Roman travelers found now a language spoken in Egypt which they could understand, and philosophers and scholars could gratify the curiosity which they had so long felt, in respect to the institutions, and monuments, and wonderful physical characteristics of the country, with safety and pleasure. In a word, the organization of a Greek government over the ancient kingdom, and the establishment of the great commercial relations of the city of Alexandria, conspired to bring Egypt out from its concealment and seclusion, and to open it in some measure to the intercourse, as well as to bring it more fully under the observation, of the rest of mankind.

Ptolemy, in fact, made it a special object of his policy to accomplish these ends. He invited Greek scholars, philosophers, poets, and artists, in great numbers, to come to Alexandria, and to make his capital their abode. He collected an immense library, which subsequently, under the name of the Alexandrian library, became one of the most celebrated collections of books and manuscripts that was ever made. We shall have occasion to refer more particularly to this library in the next chapter.

Besides prosecuting these splendid schemes for the aggrandizement of Egypt, King Ptolemy was engaged, during almost the whole period of his reign, in waging incessant wars with the surrounding nations. He engaged in these wars, in part, for the purpose of extending the boundaries of his empire, and in part for self-defense against the aggressions and encroachments of other powers. He finally succeeded in establishing his kingdom on the most stable and permanent basis, and then, when he was drawing toward the close of his life, being in fact over eighty years of age, he abdicated his throne in favor of his youngest son, whose name was also Ptolemy. Ptolemy the father, the founder of the dynasty, is known commonly in history by the name of Ptolemy Soter. His son is called Ptolemy Philadelphus. This son, though the youngest, was preferred to his brothers as heir to the throne on account of his being the son of the most favored and beloved of the monarch's wives. The determination of Soter to abdicate the throne himself arose from his wish to put this favorite son in secure possession of it before his death, in order to prevent the older brothers from disputing the succession. The coronation of Philadelphus was made one of the most magnificent and imposing ceremonies that royal pomp and parade ever arranged. Two years afterward Ptolemy the father died, and was buried by his son with a magnificence almost equal to that of his own coronation. His body was deposited in a splendid mausoleum, which had been built for the remains of Alexander; and so high was the veneration which was felt by mankind for the greatness of his exploits and the splendor of his reign, that divine honors were paid to his memory. Such was the origin of the great dynasty of the Ptolemies.

Some of the early sovereigns of the line followed in some degree the honorable example set them by the distinguished founder of it; but this example was soon lost, and was succeeded by the most extreme degeneracy and debasement. The successive sovereigns began soon to live and to reign solely for the gratification of their own sensual propensities and passions. Sensuality begins sometimes with kindness, but it ends always in the most reckless and intolerable cruelty. The Ptolemies became, in the end, the most abominable and terrible tyrants that the principle of absolute and irresponsible power ever produced. There was one vice in particular, a vice which they seem to have adopted from the Asiatic nations of the Persian empire, that resulted in the most awful consequences. This vice was incest.

The law of God, proclaimed not only in the Scriptures, but in the native instincts of the human soul, forbids intermarriages among those connected by close ties of consanguinity. The necessity for such a law rests on considerations which can not here be fully explained. They are considerations, however, which arise from causes inherent in the very nature of man as a social being, and which are of universal, perpetual, and insurmountable force. To guard his creatures against the deplorable consequences, both physical and moral, which result from the practice of such marriages, the great Author of Nature has implanted in every mind an instinctive sense of their criminality, powerful enough to give effectual warning of the danger, and so universal as to cause a distinct condemnation of them to be recorded in almost every code of written law that has ever been promulgated among mankind. The Persian sovereigns were, however, above all law, and every species of incestuous marriage was practiced by them without shame. The Ptolemies followed their example.

One of the most striking exhibitions of the nature of incestuous domestic life which is afforded by the whole dismal panorama of pagan vice and crime, is presented in the history of the great-grandfather of the Cleopatra who is the principal subject of this narrative. He was Ptolemy Physcon, the seventh in the line. It is necessary to give some particulars of his history and that of his family, in order to explain the circumstances under which Cleopatra herself came upon the stage. The name Physcon, which afterward became his historical designation, was originally given him in contempt and derision. He was very small of stature in respect to height, but his gluttony and sensuality had made him immensely corpulent in body, so that he looked more like a monster than a man. The term Physcon was a Greek word, which denoted opprobriously the ridiculous figure that he made.

The circumstances of Ptolemy Physcon's accession to the throne afford not only a striking illustration of his character, but a very faithful though terrible picture of the manners and morals of the times. He had been engaged in a long and cruel war with his brother, who was king before him, in which war he had perpetrated all imaginable atrocities, when at length his brother died, leaving as his survivors his wife, who was also his sister, and a son who was yet a child. This son was properly the heir to the crown. Physcon himself, being a brother, had no claim, as against a son. The name of the queen was Cleopatra. This was, in fact, a very common name among the princesses of the Ptolemaic line. Cleopatra, besides her son, had a daughter, who was at this time a young and beautiful girl. Her name was also Cleopatra. She was, of course, the niece, as her mother was the sister, of Physcon.

The plan of Cleopatra the mother, after her husband's death, was to make her son the king of Egypt, and to govern herself, as regent, until he should become of age. The friends and adherents of Physcon, however, formed a strong party in *his* favor. They sent for him to come to Alexandria to assert his claims to the throne. He came, and a new civil war was on the point of breaking out between the brother and sister, when at length the dispute was settled by a treaty, in which it was stipulated that Physcon should marry Cleopatra, and be king; but that he should make the son of Cleopatra by her former husband his heir. This treaty was carried into effect so far as the celebration of the marriage with the mother was concerned, and the establishment of Physcon upon the throne. But the perfidious monster, instead of keeping his faith in respect to the boy, determined to murder him; and so open and brutal were his habits of violence and cruelty, that he undertook to perpetrate the deed himself, in open day. The boy fled shrieking to the mother's arms for protection, and Physcon stabbed and killed him there, exhibiting the spectacle of a newly-married husband murdering the son of his wife in her very arms!

It is easy to conceive what sort of affection would exist between a husband and a wife after such transactions as these. In fact, there had been no love between them from the beginning. The marriage had been solely a political arrangement. Physcon hated his wife, and had murdered her son, and then, as if to complete the exhibition of the brutal lawlessness and capriciousness of his passions, he ended with falling in love with her daughter. The beautiful girl looked upon this heartless monster, as ugly and deformed in body as he was in mind, with absolute horror. But she was wholly in his power. He compelled her, by violence, to submit to his will. He repudiated the mother, and forced the daughter to become his wife.

Physcon displayed the same qualities of brutal tyranny and cruelty in the treatment of his subjects that he manifested in his own domestic relations. The particulars we can not here give, but can only say that his atrocities became at length absolutely intolerable, and a revolt so formidable broke out, that he fled from the country. In fact he barely escaped with his life, as the mob had surrounded the palace and were setting it on fire, intending to burn the tyrant himself and all the accomplices of his crimes together. Physcon, however, contrived to make his escape. He fled to the island of Cyprus, taking with him a certain beautiful boy, his son by the Cleopatra whom he had divorced; for they had been married long enough before the divorce, to have a son. The name of this boy was Memphitis. His mother was very tenderly attached to him, and Physcon took him away on this very account, to keep him as a hostage for his mother's good behavior. He fancied that, when he was gone, she might possibly attempt to resume possession of the throne.

His expectations in this respect were realized. The people of Alexandria rallied around Cleopatra, and called upon her to take the crown. She did so, feeling, perhaps, some misgivings in respect to the danger which such a step might possibly bring upon her absent boy. She quieted herself, however, by the thought that he was in the hands of his own father, and that he could not possibly come to harm.

After some little time had elapsed, and Cleopatra was beginning to be well established in her possession of the supreme power at Alexandria, her birth-day approached, and arrangements were made for celebrating it in the most magnificent manner. When the day arrived, the whole city was given up to festivities and rejoicing. Grand entertainments were given in the palace, and games, spectacles, and plays in every variety, were exhibited and performed in all quarters of the city. Cleopatra herself was enjoying amagnificent entertainment, given to the lords and ladies of the court and the officers of her army, in one of the royal palaces.

In the midst of this scene of festivity and pleasure, it was announced to the queen that a large box had arrived for her. The box was brought into the apartment. It had the appearance of containing some magnificent present, sent in at that time by some friend in honor of the occasion. The curiosity of the queen was excited to know what the mysterious coffer might contain. She ordered it to be opened; and the guests gathered around, each eager to obtain the first glimpse of the contents. The lid was removed, and a cloth beneath it was raised, when, to the unutterable horror of all who witnessed the spectacle, there was seen the head and hands of Cleopatra's beautiful boy, lying among masses of human flesh, which consisted of the rest of his body cut into pieces. The head had been left entire, that the wretched mother might recognize in the pale and lifeless features the countenance of her son. Physcon had sent the box to Alexandria, with orders that it should be retained until the evening of the birth-day, and then presented publicly to Cleopatra in the midst of the festivities of the scene. The shrieks and cries with which she filled the apartments of the palace at the first sight of the dreadful spectacle, and the agony of long-continued and inconsolable grief which followed, showed how well the cruel contrivance of the tyrant was fitted to accomplish its end.

It gives us no pleasure to write, and we are sure it can give our readers no pleasure to peruse, such shocking stories of bloody cruelty as these. It is necessary, however, to a just appreciation of the character of the great subject of this history, that we should understand the nature of the domestic influences that reigned in the family from which she sprung. In fact, it is due, as a matter of simple justice to her, that we should know what these influences were, and what were the examples set before her in her early life; since the privileges and advantages which the young enjoy in their early years, and, on the other hand, the evil influences under which they suffer, are to be taken very seriously into the account when we are passing judgment upon the follies and sins into which they subsequently fall.

The monster Physcon lived, it is true, two or three generations before the great Cleopatra; but the character of the intermediate generations, until the time of her birth, continued much the same. In fact, the cruelty, corruption, and vice which reigned in every branch of the royal family increased rather than diminished. The beautiful niece of Physcon, who, at the time of her compulsory marriage with him, evinced such an aversion to the monster, had become, at the period of her husband's death, as great a monster of ambition, selfishness, and cruelty as he. She had two sons, Lathyrus and Alexander. Physcon, when he died, left the kingdom of Egypt to her by will, authorizing her to associate with her in the government whichever of these two sons she might choose. The oldest was best entitled to this privilege, by his priority of birth; but she preferred the youngest, as she thought that her own power would be more absolute in reigning in conjunction with him, since he would be more completely under her control. The leading powers, however, in Alexandria, resisted this plan, and insisted on Cleopatra's associating her oldest son, Lathyrus, with her in the government of the realm. They compelled her to recall Lathyrus from the banishment into which she had sent him, and to put him nominally upon the throne. Cleopatra yielded to this necessity, but she forced her son to repudiate his wife, and to take, instead, another woman, whom she fancied she could make more subservient to her will. The mother and the son went on together for a time, Lathyrus being nominally king, though her determination that she would rule, and his struggles to resist her intolerable tyranny, made their wretched household the scene of terrible and perpetual quarrels. At last Cleopatra seized a number of Lathyrus's servants, the eunuchs who were employed in various offices about the palace, and after wounding and mutilating them in a horrible manner, she exhibited them to the populace, saying that it was Lathyrus that had inflicted the cruel injuries upon the sufferers, and calling upon them to arise and punish him for his crimes. In this and in other similar ways she awakened among the people of the court and of the city such an animosity against Lathyrus, that they expelled him from the country. There followed a long series of cruel and bloody wars between the mother and the son, in the course of which each party perpetrated against the other almost every imaginable deed of atrocity and crime. Alexander, the youngest son, was so afraid of his terrible mother, that he did not dare to remain in Alexandria with her, but went into a sort of banishment of his own accord. He, however, finally returned to Egypt. His mother immediately supposed that he was intending to disturb her possession of power, and resolved to destroy him. He became acquainted with her designs, and, grown desperate by the long-continued pressure of her intolerable tyranny, he resolved to bring the anxiety and terror in which he lived to an end by killing her. This he did, and then fled the country. Lathyrus, his brother, then returned, and reigned for the rest of his days in a tolerable degree of quietness and peace. At length Lathyrus died, and left the kingdom to his son, Ptolemy Auletes, who was the great Cleopatra's father.

We can not soften the picture which is exhibited to our view in the history of this celebrated family, by regarding the mother of Auletes, in the masculine and merciless traits and principles which she displayed so energetically throughout her terrible career, as an exception to the general character of the princesses who appeared from time to time in the line. In ambition, selfishness, unnatural and reckless cruelty, and utter disregard of every virtuous principle and of every domestic tie, she was but the type and representative of all the rest.

She had two daughters, for example, who were the consistent and worthy followers of such a mother. A passage in the lives of these sisters illustrates very forcibly the kind of sisterly affection which prevailed in the family of the Ptolemies. The case was this:

There were two princes of Syria, a country lying northeast of the Mediterranean Sea, and so not very far from Egypt, who, though they were brothers, were in a state of most deadly hostility to each other. One had attempted to poison the other, and afterward a war had broken out between them, and all Syria was suffering from the ravages of their armies. One of the sisters, of whom we have been speaking, married one of these princes. Her name was Tryphena. After some time, but yet while the unnatural war was still raging between the two brothers, Cleopatra, the other sister—the same Cleopatra, in fact, that had been divorced from Lathyrus at the instance of his mother—espoused the other brother. Tryphena was exceedingly incensed against Cleopatra for marrying her husband's mortal foe, and the implacable hostility and hate of the sisters was thenceforth added to that which the brothers had before exhibited, to complete the display of unnatural and parricidal passion which this shameful contest presented to the world.

In fact, Tryphena from this time seemed to feel a new and highly-excited interest in the contest, from her eager desire to revenge herself on her sister. She watched the progress of it, and took an active part in pressing forward the active prosecution of the war. The party of her husband, either from this or some other causes, seemed to be gaining the day. The husband of Cleopatra was driven from one part of the country to another, and at length, in order to provide for the security of his wife, he left her in Antioch, a large and strongly-fortified city, where he supposed that she would be safe, while he himself was engaged in prosecuting the war in other quarters where his presence seemed to be required.

On learning that her sister was at Antioch, Tryphena urged her husband to attack the place. He accordingly advanced with a strong detachment of the army, and besieged and took the city. Cleopatra would, of course, have fallen into his hands as a captive; but, to escape this fate, she fled to a temple for refuge. A temple was considered, in those days, an inviolable sanctuary. The soldiers accordingly left her there. Tryphena, however, made a request that her husband would deliver the unhappy fugitive into her hands. She was determined, she said, to kill her. Her husband remonstrated with her against this atrocious proposal. "It would be a wholly useless act of cruelty," said he, "to destroy her life. She can do us no possible harm in the future progress of the war, while to murder her under these circumstances will only exasperate her husband and her friends, and nerve them with new strength for the remainder of the contest. And then, besides, she has taken refuge in a temple; and if we violate that sanctuary, we shall incur, by such an act of sacrilege, the implacable displeasure of Heaven. Consider, too, that she is your sister, and for you to kill her would be to commit an unnatural and wholly inexcusable crime."

So saying, he commanded Tryphena to say no more upon the subject, for he would on no account consent that Cleopatra should suffer any injury whatever.

This refusal on the part of her husband to comply with her request only inflamed Tryphena's insane resentment and anger the more. In fact, the earnestness with which he espoused her sister's cause, and the interest which he seemed to feel in her fate, aroused Tryphena's jealousy. She believed, or pretended to believe, that her husband was influenced by a sentiment of love in so warmly defending her. The object of her hate, from being simply an enemy, became now, in her view, a rival, and she resolved that, at all hazards, she should be destroyed. She accordingly ordered a body of desperate soldiers to break into the temple and seize her. Cleopatra fled in terror to the altar, and clung to it with such convulsive force that the soldiers cut her hands off before they could tear her away, and then, maddened by her resistance and the sight of blood, they stabbed her again and again upon the floor of the temple, where she fell. The appalling shrieks with which the wretched victim filled the air in the first moments of her flight and her terror, subsided, as her life ebbed away, into the most awful imprecations of the judgments of Heaven upon the head of the unnatural sister whose implacable hate had destroyed her.

Notwithstanding the specimens that we have thus given of the character and action of this extraordinary family, the government of this dynasty, extending, as it did, through the reigns of thirteen sovereigns and over a period of nearly three hundred years, has always been considered one of the most liberal, enlightened, and prosperous of all the governments of ancient times. We shall have something to say in the next chapter in respect to the internal condition of the country while these violent men were upon the throne. In the mean time, we will here only add, that whoever is inclined, in observing the ambition, the selfishness, the party spirit, the unworthy intrigues, and the irregularities of moral conduct, which modern rulers and statesmen sometimes exhibit to mankind in their personal and political career, to believe in a retrogression and degeneracy of national character as the world advances in age, will be very effectually undeceived by reading attentively a full history of this celebrated dynasty, and reflecting, as he reads, that the narrative presents, on the whole, a fair and honest exhibition of the general character of the men by whom, in ancient times, the world was governed.

CHAPTER III.

ALEXANDRIA.

Internal administration of the Ptolemies.—Industry of the people.—Its happy effects.—Idleness the parent of vice.—An idle aristocracy generally vicious. —Degradation and vice.—Employment a cure for both.—Greatness of Alexandria.—Situation of its port.—Warehouses and granaries.—Business of the port.—Scenes within the city.—The natives protected in their industry.— Public edifices.—The light-house.—Fame of the light-house.—Its conspicuous position.—Mode of lighting the tower.—Modern method—The architect of the Pharos.—His ingenious stratagem.—Ruins of the Pharos.— The Alexandrian library.—Immense magnitude of the library.—The Serapion. —The Serapis of Egypt.—The Serapis of Greece.—Ptolemy's dream.— Importance of the statue.—Ptolemy's proposal to the King of Sinope.—His ultimate success.—Mode of obtaining books.—The Jewish Scriptures.— Seclusion of the Jews.—Interest felt in their Scriptures.—Jewish slaves in Egypt.—Ptolemy's designs.—Ptolemy liberates the slaves.—Their ransom paid.—Ptolemy's success.—The Septuagint.—Early copies of the Septuagint. —Present copies.—Various other plans of the Ptolemies.—Means of raising money.—Heavy taxes.—Poverty of the people.—Ancient and modern capitals.—Liberality of the Ptolemies.—Splendor and renown of Alexandria. —Her great rival.

It must not be imagined by the reader that the scenes of vicious indulgence, and reckless cruelty and crime, which were exhibited with such dreadful frequency, and carried to such an enormous excess in the palaces of the Egyptian kings, prevailed to the same extent throughout the mass of the community during the period of their reign. The internal administration of government, and the institutions by which the industrial pursuits of the mass of the people were regulated, and peace and order preserved, and justice enforced between man and man, were all this time in the hands of men well qualified, on the whole, for the trusts committed to their charge, and in a good degree faithful in the performance of their duties; and thus the ordinary affairs of government, and the general routine of domestic and social life, went on, notwithstanding the profligacy of the kings, in a course of very tolerable peace, prosperity, and happiness. During every one of the three hundred years over which the history of the Ptolemies extends, the whole length and breadth of the land of Egypt exhibited, with comparatively few interruptions, one wide-spread scene of busy industry. The inundations came at their appointed season, and then regularly retired. The boundless fields which the waters had fertilized were then every where tilled. The lands were plowed; the seed was sown; the canals and water-courses, which ramified from the river in every direction over the ground, were opened or closed, as the case required, to regulate the irrigation. The inhabitants were busy, and, consequently, they were virtuous. And as the sky of Egypt is seldom or never darkened by clouds and storms, the scene presented to the eye the same unchanging aspect of smiling verdure and beauty, day after day, and month after month, until the ripened grain was gathered into the store-houses, and the land was cleared for another inundation.

We say that the people were virtuous because they were busy; for there is no principle of political economy more fully established than that vice in the social state is the incident and symptom of idleness. It prevails always in those classes of every great population who are either released by the possession of fixed and unchangeable wealth from the necessity, or excluded by their poverty and degradation from the advantage, of useful employment. Wealth that is free, and subject to its possessor's control, so that he can, if he will, occupy himself in the management of it, while it sometimes may make individuals vicious, does not generally corrupt classes of men, for it does not make them idle. But wherever the institutions of a country are such as to create an aristocratic class, whose incomes depend on entailed estates, or on fixed and permanent annuities, so that the capital on which they live can not afford them any mental occupation, they are doomed necessarily to inaction and idleness. Vicious pleasures and indulgences are, with such a class as a whole, the inevitable result; for the innocent enjoyments of man are planned and designed by the Author of Nature only for the intervals of rest and repose in a life of activity. They are always found wholly insufficient to satisfy one who makes pleasure the whole end and aim of his being.

In the same manner, if, either from the influence of the social institutions of a country, or from the operation of natural causes which human power is unable to control, there is a class of men too low, and degraded, and miserable to be reached by the ordinary inducements to daily toil, so certain are they to grow corrupt and depraved, that degradation has become in all languages a term almost synonymous with vice. There are many exceptions, it is true, to these general laws. Many active men are very wicked; and there have been frequent instances of the most exalted virtue among nobles and kings. Still, as a general law, it is unquestionably true that vice is the incident of idleness; and the sphere of vice, therefore, is at the top and at the bottom of society—those being the regions in which idleness reigns. The great remedy, too, for vice is employment. To make a community virtuous, it is essential that all ranks and gradations of it, from the highest to the lowest, should have something to do.

In accordance with these principles, we observe that, while the most extreme and abominable wickedness seemed to hold continual and absolute sway in the palaces of the Ptolemies, and among the nobles of their courts, the working ministers of state, and the men on whom the actual governmental functions devolved, discharged their duties with wisdom and fidelity, and throughout all the ordinary ranks and gradations of society there prevailed generally a very considerable degree of industry, prosperity and happiness. This prosperity prevailed not only in the rural districts of the Delta and along the valley of the Nile, but also among the merchants, and navigators, and artisans of Alexandria.

Alexandria became, in fact, very soon after it was founded, a very great and busy city. Many things conspired to make it at once a great commercial emporium. In the first place, it was the depot of export for all the surplus grain and other agricultural produce which was raised in such abundance along the Egyptian valley. This produce was brought down in boats to the upper point of the Delta, where the branches of the river divided, and thence down the Canopic branch to the city. The city was not, in fact, situated directly upon this branch, but upon a narrow tongue of land, at a little distance from it, near the sea. It was not easy to enter the channel directly, on account of the bars and sand-banks at its mouth, produced by the eternal conflict between the waters of the river and the surges of the sea. The water was deep, however, as Alexander's engineers had discovered, at the place where the city was built, and, by establishing the port there, and then cutting a canal across to the Nile, they were enabled to bring the river and the sea at once into easy communication.

The produce of the valley was thus brought down the river and through the canal to the city. Here immense warehouses and granaries were erected for its reception, that it might be safely preserved until the ships that came into the port were ready to take it away. These ships came from Syria, from all the coasts of Asia Minor, from Greece, and from Rome. They brought the agricultural productions of their own countries, as well as articles of manufacture of various kinds; these they sold to the merchants of Alexandria, and purchased the productions of Egypt in return.

The port of Alexandria presented thus a constant picture of life and animation. Merchant ships were continually coming and going, or lying at anchor in the roadstead. Seamen were hoisting sails, or raising anchors, or rowing their capacious galleys through the water, singing, as they pulled, to the motion of the oars. Within the city there was the same ceaseless activity. Here groups of men were unloading the canal boats which had arrived from the river. There porters were transporting bales of merchandise or sacks of grain from a warehouse to a pier, or from one landing to another. The occasional parading of the king's guards, or the arrival and departure of ships of war to land or to take away bodies of armed men, were occurrences that sometimes intervened to interrupt, or as perhaps the people then would have said, to adorn this scene of useful industry; and now and then, for a brief period, these peaceful vocations would be wholly suspended and set aside by a revolt or by a civil war, waged by rival brothers against each other, or instigated by the conflicting claims of a mother and son. These interruptions, however, were comparatively few, and, in ordinary cases, not of long continuance. It was for the interest of all branches of the royal line to do as little injury as possible to the commercial and agricultural operations of the realm. In fact, it was on the prosperity of those operations that the revenues depended. The rulers were well aware of this, and so, however implacably two rival princes may have hated one another, and however desperately each party may have struggled to destroy all active combatants whom they should find in arms against them, they were both under every possible inducement to spare the private property and the lives of the peaceful population. This population, in fact, engaged thus in profitable industry, constituted, with the avails of their labors, the very estate for which the combatants were contending.

Seeing the subject in this light, the Egyptian sovereigns, especially Alexander and the earlier Ptolemies, made every effort in their power to promote the commercial greatness of Alexandria. They built palaces, it is true, but they also built warehouses.

One of the most expensive and celebrated of all the edifices that they reared was the light-house which has been already alluded to. This light-house was a lofty tower, built of white marble. It was situated upon the island of Pharos, opposite to the city, and at some distance from it. There was a sort of isthmus of shoals and sand-bars connecting the island with the shore. Over these shallows a pier or causeway was built, which finally became a broad and inhabited neck. The principal part of the ancient city, however, was on the main land.

The curvature of the earth requires that a light-house on a coast should have a considerable elevation, otherwise its summit would not appear above the horizon, unless the mariner were very near. To attain this elevation, the architects usually take advantage of some hill or cliff, or rocky eminence near the shore. There was, however, no opportunity to do this at Pharos; for the island was, like the main land, level and low. The requisite elevation could only be attained, therefore, by the masonry of an edifice, and the blocks of marble necessary for the work had to be brought from a great distance. The Alexandrian light-house was reared in the time of Ptolemy Philadelphus, the second monarch in the line. No pains or expense were spared in its construction. The edifice, when completed, was considered one of the seven wonders of the world. It was indebted for its fame, however, in some degree, undoubtedly to the conspicuousness of its situation, rising, as it did, at the entrance of the greatest commercial emporium of its time, and standing there, like a pillar of cloud by day and of fire by night, to attract the welcome gaze of every wandering mariner whose ship came within its horizon, and to awaken his gratitude by tendering him its guidance and dispelling his fears.

The light at the top of the tower was produced by a fire, made of such combustibles as would emit the brightest flame. This fire burned slowly through the day, and then was kindled up anew when the sun went down, and was continually replenished through the night with fresh supplies of fuel. In modern times, a much more convenient and economical mode is adopted to produce the requisite illumination. A great blazing lamp burns brilliantly in the center of the lantern of the tower, and all that part of the radiation from the flame which would naturally have beamed upward, or downward, or laterally, or back toward the land, is so turned by a curious system of reflectors and polyzonal lenses, most ingeniously contrived and very exactly adjusted, as to be thrown forward in one broad and thin, but brilliant sheet of light, which shoots out where its radiance is needed, over the surface of the sea. Before these inventions were perfected, far the largest portion of the light emitted by the illumination of light-house towers streamed away wastefully in landward directions, or was lost among the stars.

Of course, the glory of erecting such an edifice as the Pharos of Alexandria, and of maintaining it in the performance of its functions, was very great; the question might, however, very naturally arise whether this glory was justly due to the architect through whose scientific skill the work was actually accomplished, or to the monarch by whose power and resources the architect was sustained. The name of the architect was Sostratus. He was a Greek. The monarch was, as has already been stated, the second Ptolemy, called commonly Ptolemy Philadelphus. Ptolemy ordered that, in completing the tower, a marble tablet should be built into the wall, at a suitable place near the summit, and that a proper inscription should be carved upon it, with his name as the builder of the edifice conspicuous thereon. Sostratus preferred inserting his own name. He accordingly made the tablet and set it in its place. He cut the inscription upon the face of it, in Greek characters, with his own name as the author of the work. He did this secretly, and then covered the face of the tablet with an artificial composition, made with lime, to imitate the natural surface of the stone. On this outer surface he cut a new inscription, in which he inserted the name of the king. In process of time the lime moldered away, the king's inscription disappeared, and his own, which thenceforward continued as long as the building endured, came out to view.

The Pharos was said to have been four hundred feet high. It was famed throughout the world for many centuries; nothing, however, remains of it now but a heap of useless and unmeaning ruins.

Besides the light that beamed from the summit of this lofty tower, there was another center of radiance and illumination in ancient Alexandria, which was in some respects still more conspicuous and renowned, namely, an immense library and museum established and maintained by the Ptolemies. The Museum, which was first established, was not, as its name might now imply, a collection of curiosities, but an institution of learning, consisting of a body of learned men, who devoted their time to philosophical and scientific pursuits. The institution was richly endowed, and magnificent buildings were erected for its use. The king who established it began immediately to make a collection of books for the use of the members of the institution. This was attended with great expense, as every book that was added to the collection required to be transcribed with a pen on parchment or papyrus with infinite labor and care. Great numbers of scribes were constantly employed upon this work at the Museum. The kings who were most interested in forming this library would seize the books that were possessed by individual scholars, or that were deposited in the various cities of their dominions, and then, causing beautiful copies of them to be made by the scribes of the Museum, they would retain the originals for the great Alexandrian library, and give the copies to the men or the cities that had been thus despoiled. In the same manner they would borrow, as they called it, from all travelers who visited Egypt, any valuable books which they might have in their possession, and, retaining the originals, give them back copies instead.

In process of time the library increased to four hundred thousand volumes. There was then no longer any room in the buildings of the Museum for further additions. There was, however, in another part of the city, a great temple called the Serapion. This temple was a very magnificent edifice, or, rather, group of edifices, dedicated to the god Serapis. The origin and history of this temple were very remarkable. The legend was this:

It seems that one of the ancient and long-venerated gods of the Egyptians was a deity named Serapis. He had been, among other divinities, the object of Egyptian adoration ages before Alexandria was built or the Ptolemies reigned. There was also, by a curious coincidence, a statue of the same name at a great commercial town named Sinope, which was built upon the extremity of a promontory which projected from Asia Minor into the Euxine Sea. Sinope was, in some sense, the Alexandria of the north, being the center and seat of a great portion of the commerce of that quarter of the world.

The Serapis of Sinope was considered as the protecting deity of seamen, and the navigators who came and went to and from the city made sacrifices to him, and offered him oblations and prayers, believing that they were, in a great measure, dependent upon some mysterious and inscrutable power which he exercised for their safety in storms. They carried the knowledge of his name, and tales of his imaginary interpositions, to all the places that they visited; and thus the fame of the god became extended, first, to all the coasts of the Euxine Sea, and subsequently to distant provinces and kingdoms. The Serapis of Sinope began to be considered every where as the tutelar god of seamen.

Accordingly, when the first of the Ptolemies was forming his various plans for adorning and aggrandizing Alexandria, he received, he said, one night, a divine intimation in a dream that he was to obtain the statue of Serapis from Sinope, and set it up in Alexandria, in a suitable temple which he was in the mean time to erect in honor of the god. It is obvious that very great advantages to the city would result from the accomplishment of this design. In the first place, a temple to the god Serapis would be a new distinction for it in the minds of the rural population, who would undoubtedly suppose that the deity honored by it was their own ancient god. Then the whole maritime and nautical interest of the world, which had been, accustomed to adore the god of Sinope, would turn to Alexandria as the great center of religious attraction, if their venerated idol could be carried and placed in a new and magnificent temple built expressly for him there. Alexandria could never be the chief naval port and station of the world, unless it contained the sanctuary and shrine of the god of seamen.

Ptolemy sent accordingly to the King of Sinope and proposed to purchase the idol. The embassage was, however, unsuccessful. The king refused to give up the god. The negotiations were continued for two years, but all in vain. At length, on account of some failure in the regular course of the seasons on that coast, there was a famine there, which became finally so severe that the people of the city were induced to consent to give up their deity to the Egyptians in exchange for a supply of corn. Ptolemy sent the corn and received the idol. He then built the temple, which, when finished, surpassed in grandeur and magnificence almost every sacred structure in the world.

It was in this temple that the successive additions to the Alexandrian library were deposited, when the apartments of the Museum became full. In the end there were four hundred thousand rolls or volumes in the Museum, and three hundred thousand in the Serapion. The former was called the parent library, and the latter, being, as it were, the offspring of the first, was called the daughter.

Ptolemy Philadelphus, who interested himself very greatly in collecting this library, wished to make it a complete collection of all the books in the world. He employed scholars to read and study, and travelers to make extensive tours, for the purpose of learning what books existed among all the surrounding nations; and, when he learned of their existence, he spared no pains or expense in attempting to procure either the originals themselves, or the most perfect and authentic copies of them. He sent to Athens and obtained the works of the most celebrated Greek historians, and then causing, as in other cases, most beautiful transcripts to be made, he sent the transcripts back to Athens, and a very large sum of money with them as an equivalent for the difference of value between originals and copies in such an exchange.

In the course of the inquiries which Ptolemy made into the literature of the surrounding nations, in his search for accessions to his library, he heard that the Jews had certain sacred writings in their temple at Jerusalem, comprising a minute and extremely interesting history of their nation from the earliest periods, and also many other books of sacred prophecy and poetry. These books, which were, in fact, the Hebrew Scriptures of the Old Testament, were then wholly unknown to all nations except the Jews, and among the Jews were known only to priests and scholars. They were kept sacred at Jerusalem. The Jews would have considered them as profaned in being exhibited to the view of pagan nations. In fact, the learned men of other countries would not have been able to read them; for the Jews secluded themselves so closely from the rest of mankind, that their language was, in that age, scarcely ever heard beyond the confines of Judea and Galilee.

Ptolemy very naturally thought that a copy of these sacred books would be a great acquisition to his library. They constituted, in fact, the whole literature of a nation which was, in some respects, the most extraordinary that ever existed on the globe. Ptolemy conceived the idea, also, of not only adding to his library a copy of these writings in the original Hebrew, but of causing a translation of them to be made into Greek, so that they might easily be read by the Greek and Roman scholars who were drawn in great numbers to his capital by the libraries and the learned institutions which he had established there. The first thing to be effected, however, in accomplishing either of these plans, was to obtain the consent of the Jewish authorities. They would probably object to giving up any copy of their sacred writings at all.

There was one circumstance which led Ptolemy to imagine that the Jews would, at that time particularly, be averse to granting any request of such a nature coming from an Egyptian king, and that was, that during certain wars which had taken place in previous reigns, a considerable number of prisoners had been taken by the Egyptians, and had been brought to Egypt as captives, where they had been sold to the inhabitants, and were now scattered over the land as slaves. They were employed as servile laborers in tilling the fields, or in turning enormous wheels to pump up water from the Nile. The masters of these hapless bondmen conceived, like other slave-holders, that they had a right of property in their slaves. This was in some respects true, since they had bought them of the government at the close of the war for a consideration; and though they obviously derived from this circumstance no valid proprietary right or claim as against the men personally, it certainly would seem that it gave them a just claim against the government of whom they bought, in case of subsequent manumission.

Ptolemy or his minister, for it can not now be known who was the real actor in these transactions, determined on liberating these slaves and sending them back to their native land, as a means of propitiating the Jews and inclining them to listen favorably to the request which he was about to prefer for a copy of their sacred writings. He, however, paid to those who held the captives a very liberal sum for ransom. The ancient historians, who never allow the interest of their narratives to suffer for want of a proper amplification on their part of the scale on which the deeds which they record were performed, say that the number of slaves liberated on this occasion was a hundred and twenty thousand, and the sum paid for them, as compensation to the owners, was six hundred talents, equal to six hundred thousand dollars.[1]

[Footnote 1: It will be sufficiently accurate for the general reader of history to consider the Greek talent, referred to in such transactions as these, as equal in English money to two hundred and fifty pounds, in American to a thousand dollars. It is curious to observe that, large as the total was that was paid for the liberation of these slaves, the amount paid for each individual was, after all, only a sum equal to about five dollars.]

And yet this was only a preliminary expense to pave the way for the acquisition of a single series of books, to add to the variety of the immense collection.

After the liberation and return of the captives, Ptolemy sent a splendid embassage to Jerusalem, with very respectful letters to the high priest, and with very magnificent presents. The embassadors were received with the highest honors. The request of Ptolemy that he should be allowed to take a copy of the sacred books for his library was very readily granted. The priests caused copies to be made of all the sacred writings. These copies were executed in the most magnificent style, and were splendidly illuminated with letters of gold. The Jewish government also, at Ptolemy's request, designated a company of Hebrew scholars, six from each tribe—men learned in both the Greek and Hebrew languages—to proceed to Alexandria, and there, at the Museum, to make a careful translation of the Hebrew books into Greek. As there were twelve tribes, and six translators chosen from each, there were seventy-two translators in all. They made their translation, and it was called the *Septuagint*, from the Latin *septuaginta duo*, which means seventy-two.

Although out of Judea there was no feeling of reverence for these Hebrew Scriptures as books of divine authority, there was still a strong interest felt in them as very entertaining and curious works of history, by all the Greek and Roman scholars who frequented Alexandria to study at the Museum. Copies were accordingly made of the Septuagint translation, and were taken to other countries; and there, in process of time, copies of the copies were made, until at length the work became extensively circulated throughout the whole learned world. When, finally, Christianity became extended over the Roman empire, the priests and monks looked with even a stronger interest than the ancient scholars had felt upon this early translation of so important a portion of the sacred Scriptures. They made new copies for abbeys, monasteries, and colleges; and when, at length, the art of printing was discovered, this work was one of the first on which the magic power of typography was tried. The original manuscript made by the scribes of the seventy-two, and all the early transcripts which were made from it, have long since been lost or destroyed; but, instead of them, we have now hundreds of thousands of copies in compact printed volumes, scattered among the public and private libraries of Christendom. In fact, now, after the lapse of two thousand years, a copy of Ptolemy's Septuagint may be obtained of any considerable bookseller in any country of the civilized world; and though it required a national embassage, and an expenditure, if the accounts are true, of more than a million of dollars, originally to obtain it, it may be procured without difficulty now by two days' wages of an ordinary laborer.

Besides the building of the Pharos, the Museum, and the Temple of Serapis, the early Ptolemies formed and executed a great many other plans tending to the same ends which the erection of these splendid edifices was designed to secure, namely, to concentrate in Alexandria all possible means of attraction, commercial, literary, and religious, so as to make the city the great center of interest, and the common resort for all mankind. They raised immense revenues for these and other purposes by taxing heavily the whole agricultural produce of the valley of the Nile. The inundations, by the boundless fertility which they annually produced, supplied the royal treasuries. Thus the Abyssinian rains at the sources of the Nile built the Pharos at its mouth, and endowed the Alexandrian library.

The taxes laid upon the people of Egypt to supply the Ptolemies with funds were, in fact, so heavy, that only the bare means of subsistence were left to the mass of the agricultural population. In admiring the greatness and glory of the city, therefore, we must remember that there was a gloomy counterpart to its splendor in the very extended destitution and poverty to which the mass of the people were everywhere doomed. They lived in hamlets of wretched huts along the banks of the river, in order that the capital might be splendidly adorned with temples and palaces. They passed their lives in darkness and ignorance, that seven hundred thousand volumes of expensive manuscripts might be enrolled at the Museum for the use of foreign philosophers and scholars. The policy of the Ptolemies was, perhaps, on the whole, the best, for the general advancement and ultimate welfare of mankind, which could have been pursued in the age in which they lived and acted; but, in applauding the results which they attained, we must not wholly forget the cost which they incurred in attaining them. At the same cost, we could, at the present day, far surpass them. If the people of the United States will surrender the comforts and conveniences which they individually enjoy—if the farmers scattered in their comfortable homes on the hill-sides and plains throughout the land will give up their houses, their furniture, their carpets, their books, and the privileges of their children, and then—withholding from the produce of their annual toil only a sufficient reservation to sustain them and their families through the year, in a life like that of a beast of burden, spent in some miserable and naked hovel—send the rest to some hereditary sovereign residing upon the Atlantic sea-board, that he may build with the proceeds a splendid capital, they may have an Alexandria now that will infinitely exceed the ancient city of the Ptolemies in splendor and renown. The nation, too, would, in such a case, pay for its metropolis the same price, precisely, that the ancient Egyptians paid for theirs.

The Ptolemies expended the revenues which they raised by this taxation mainly in a very liberal and enlightened manner, for the accomplishment of the purposes which they had in view. The building of the Pharos, the removal of the statue of Serapis, and the endowment of the Museum and the library were great conceptions, and they were carried into effect in the most complete and perfect manner. All the other operations which they devised and executed for the extension and aggrandizement of the city were conceived and executed in the same spirit of scientific and enlightened liberality. Streets were opened; the most splendid palaces were built; docks, piers and breakwaters were constructed, and fortresses and towers were armed and garrisoned. Then every means was employed to attract to the city a great concourse from all the most highly-civilized nations then existing. The highest inducements were offered to merchants, mechanics, and artisans to make the city their abode. Poets, painters, sculptors, and scholars of every nation and degree were made welcome, and every facility was afforded them for the prosecution of their various pursuits. These plans were all eminently successful. Alexandria rose rapidly to the highest consideration and importance; and, at the time when Cleopatra—born to preside over this scene of magnificence and splendor— came upon the stage, the city had but one rival in the world. That rival was Rome.

CHAPTER IV.

CLEOPATRA'S FATHER.

Rome the rival of Alexandria.—Extent of their rule.—Extension of the Roman empire.—Cleopatra's father.—Ptolemy's ignoble birth.—Caesar and Pompey.—Ptolemy purchases the alliance of Rome.—Taxes to raise the money.—Revolt at Alexandria.—Ptolemy's flight.—Berenice.—Her marriage with Seleucus.—Cleopatra's early life.—Ptolemy an object of contempt.— Ptolemy's interview with Cato.—Character of Cato.—Ptolemy's reception.— Cato's advice to him.—Ptolemy arrives at Rome.—His application to Pompey.—Action of the Roman senate.—Plans for restoring Ptolemy.— Measures of Berenice.—Her embassage to Rome.—Ptolemy's treachery.—Its consequences.—Opposition to Ptolemy.—The prophecy.—Attempts to evade the oracle.—Gabinius undertakes the cause.—Mark Antony.—His history and character.—Antony in Greece.—He joins Gabinius.—Danger of crossing the deserts.—Armies destroyed.—Mark Antony's character.—His personal appearance.—March across the desert.—Pelusium taken.—March across the Delta.—Success of the Romans.—Berenice a prisoner.—Fate of Archelaus.— Grief of Antony.—Unnatural joy of Ptolemy.

When the time was approaching in which Cleopatra appeared upon the stage, Rome was perhaps the only city that could be considered as the rival of Alexandria, in the estimation of mankind, in respect to interest and attractiveness as a capital. In one respect, Rome was vastly superior to the Egyptian metropolis, and that was in the magnitude and extent of the military power which it wielded among the nations of the earth. Alexandria ruled over Egypt, and over a few of the neighboring coasts and islands; but in the course of the three centuries during which she had been acquiring her greatness and fame, the Roman empire had extended itself over almost the whole civilized world. Egypt had been, thus far, too remote to be directly reached; but the affairs of Egypt itself became involved at length with the operations of the Roman power, about the time of Cleopatra's birth, in a very striking and peculiar manner; and as the consequences of the transaction were the means of turning the whole course of the queen's subsequent history, a narration of it is necessary to a proper understanding of the circumstances under which she commenced her career. In fact, it was the extension of the Roman empire to the limits of Egypt, and the connections which thence arose between the leading Roman generals and the Egyptian sovereign, which have made the story of this particular queen so much more conspicuous, as an object of interest and attention to mankind, than that of any other one of the ten Cleopatras who rose successively in the same royal line.

Ptolemy Auletes, Cleopatra's father, was perhaps, in personal character, the most dissipated, degraded, and corrupt of all the sovereigns in the dynasty. He spent his whole time in vice and debauchery. The only honest accomplishment that he seemed to possess was his skill in playing upon the flute; of this he was very vain. He instituted musical contests, in which the musical performers of Alexandria played for prizes and crowns; and he himself was accustomed to enter the lists with the rest as a competitor. The people of Alexandria, and the world in general, considered such pursuits as these wholly unworthy the attention of the representative of so illustrious a line of sovereigns, and the abhorrence which they felt for the monarch's vices and crimes was mingled with a feeling of contempt for the meanness of his ambition.

There was a doubt in respect to his title to the crown, for his birth, on the mother's side, was irregular and ignoble. Instead, however, of attempting to confirm and secure his possession of power by a vigorous and prosperous administration of the government, he wholly abandoned all concern in respect to the course of public affairs; and then, to guard against the danger of being deposed, he conceived the plan of getting himself recognized at Rome as one of the allies of the Roman people. If this were once done, he supposed that the Roman government would feel under an obligation to sustain him on his throne in the event of any threatened danger.

The Roman government was a sort of republic, and the two most powerful men in the state at this time were Pompey and Caesar. Caesar was in the ascendency at Rome at the time that Ptolemy made his application for an alliance. Pompey was absent in Asia Minor, being engaged in prosecuting a war with Mithradates, a very powerful monarch, who was at that time resisting the Roman power. Caesar was very deeply involved in debt, and was, moreover, very much in need of money, not only for relief from existing embarrassments, but as a means of subsequent expenditure, to enable him to accomplish certain great political schemes which he was entertaining. After many negotiations and delays, it was agreed that Caesar would exert his influence to secure an alliance between the Roman people and Ptolemy, on condition that Ptolemy paid him the sum of six thousand talents, equal to about six millions of dollars. A part of the money, Caesar said, was for Pompey.

The title of ally was conferred, and Ptolemy undertook to raise the money which he had promised by increasing the taxes of his kingdom. The measures, however, which he thus adopted for the purpose of making himself the more secure in his possession of the throne, proved to be the means of overthrowing him. The discontent and disaffection of his people, which had been strong and universal before, though suppressed and concealed, broke out now into open violence. That there should be laid upon them, in addition to all their other burdens, these new oppressions, heavier than those which they had endured before, and exacted for such a purpose too, was not to be endured. To be compelled to see their country sold on any terms to the Roman people was sufficiently hard to bear; but to be forced to raise, themselves, and pay the price of the transfer, was absolutely intolerable. Alexandria commenced a revolt. Ptolemy was not a man to act decidedly against such a demonstration, or, in fact, to evince either calmness or courage in any emergency whatever. His first thought was to escape from Alexandria to save his life. His second, to make the best of his way to Rome, to call upon the Roman people to come to the succor of their ally!

Ptolemy left five children behind him in his flight The eldest was the Princess Berenice, who had already reached maturity. The second was the great Cleopatra, the subject of this history. Cleopatra was, at this time, about eleven years old. There were also two sons, but they were very young. One of them was named Ptolemy.

The Alexandrians determined on raising Berenice to the throne in her father's place, as soon as his flight was known. They thought that the sons were too young to attempt to reign in such an emergency, as it was very probable that Auletes, the father, would attempt to recover his kingdom. Berenice very readily accepted the honor and power which were offered to her. She established herself in her father's palace, and began her reign in great magnificence and splendor. In process of time she thought that her position would be strengthened by a marriage with a royal prince from some neighboring realm. She first sent embassadors to make proposals to a prince

36

of Syria named Antiochus. The embassadors came back, bringing word that Antiochus was dead, but that he had a brother named Seleucus, upon whom the succession fell. Berenice then sent them back to make the same offers to him. He accepted the proposals, came to Egypt, and he and Berenice were married. After trying him for a while, Berenice found that, for some reason or other, she did not like him as a husband, and, accordingly she caused him to be strangled.

At length, after various other intrigues and much secret management, Berenice succeeded in a second negotiation, and married a prince, or a pretended prince, from some country of Asia Minor, whose name was Archelaus. She was better pleased with this second husband than she had been with the first, and she began, at last, to feel somewhat settled and established on her throne, and to be prepared, as she thought, to offer effectual resistance to her father in case he should ever attempt to return.

It was in the midst of the scenes, and surrounded by the influences which might be expected to prevail in the families of such a father and such a sister, that Cleopatra spent those years of life in which the character is formed. During all these revolutions, and exposed to all these exhibitions of licentious wickedness, and of unnatural cruelty and crime, she was growing up in the royal palaces a spirited and beautiful, but indulged and neglected child.

In the mean time, Auletes, the father, went on toward Rome. So far as his character and his story were known among the surrounding nations, he was the object of universal obloquy, both on account of his previous career of degrading vice, and now, still more, for this ignoble flight from the difficulties in which his vices and crimes had involved him.

He stopped, on the way, at the island of Rhodes. It happened that Cato, the great Roman philosopher and general, was at Rhodes at this time. Cato was a man of stern, unbending virtue, and of great influence at that period in public affairs. Ptolemy sent a messenger to inform Cato of his arrival, supposing, of course, that the Roman general would hasten, on hearing of the fact, to pay his respects to so great a personage as he, a king of Egypt—a Ptolemy— though suffering under a temporary reverse of fortune. Cato directed the messenger to reply that, so far as he was aware, he had no particular business with Ptolemy. "Say, however, to the king," he added, "that, if he has any business with me, he may call and see me, if he pleases."

Ptolemy was obliged to suppress his resentment and submit. He thought it very essential to the success of his plans that he should see Cato, and secure, if possible, his interest and co-operation; and he consequently made preparations for paying, instead of receiving, the visit, intending to go in the greatest royal state that he could command. He accordingly appeared at

Cato's lodgings on the following day, magnificently dressed, and accompanied by many attendants. Cato, who was dressed in the plainest and most simple manner, and whose apartment was furnished in a style corresponding with the severity of his character, did not even rise when the king entered the room. He simply pointed with his hand, and bade the visitor take a seat.

Ptolemy began to make a statement of his case, with a view to obtaining Cato's influence with the Roman people to induce them to interpose in his behalf. Cato, however, far from evincing any disposition to espouse his visitor's cause, censured him, in the plainest terms, for having abandoned his proper position in his own kingdom, to go and make himself a victim and a prey for the insatiable avarice of the Roman leaders. "You can do nothing at Rome," he said, "but by the influence of bribes; and all the resources of Egypt will not be enough to satisfy the Roman greediness for money." He concluded by recommending him to go back to Alexandria, and rely for his hopes of extrication from the difficulties which surrounded him on the exercise of his own energy and resolution there.

Ptolemy was greatly abashed at this rebuff, but, on consultation with his attendants and followers, it was decided to be too late now to return. The whole party accordingly re-embarked on board their galleys, and pursued their way to Rome.

Ptolemy found, on his arrival at the city, that Caesar was absent in Gaul, while Pompey, on the other hand, who had returned victorious from his campaigns against Mithradates, was now the great leader of influence and power at the Capitol. This change of circumstances was not, however, particularly unfavorable; for Ptolemy was on friendly terms with Pompey, as he had been with Caesar. He had assisted him in his wars with Mithradates by sending him a squadron of horse, in pursuance of his policy of cultivating friendly relations with the Roman people by every means in his power. Besides, Pompey had received a part of the money which Ptolemy had paid to Caesar as the price of the Roman alliance, and was to receive his share of the rest in case Ptolemy should ever be restored. Pompey was accordingly interested in favoring the royal fugitive's cause. He received him in his palace, entertained him in magnificent style, and took immediate measures for bringing his cause before the Roman Senate, urging upon that body the adoption of immediate and vigorous measures for effecting his restoration, as an ally whom they were bound to protect against his rebellious subjects. There was at first some opposition in the Roman Senate against espousing the cause of such a man, but it was soon put down, being overpowered in part by Pompey's authority, and in part silenced by Ptolemy's promises and bribes. The Senate determined to restore the king to his throne, and began to make arrangements for carrying the measure into effect.

The Roman provinces nearest to Egypt were Cilicia and Syria, countries situated on the eastern and northeastern coast of the Mediterranean Sea, north of Judea. The forces stationed in these provinces would be, of course, the most convenient for furnishing the necessary troops for the expedition. The province of Cilicia was under the command of the consul Lentulus. Lentulus was at this time at Rome; he had repaired to the capital for some temporary purpose, leaving his province and the troops stationed there under the command, for the time, of a sort of lieutenant general named Gabinius. It was concluded that this Lentulus, with his Syrian forces, should undertake the task of reinstating Ptolemy on his throne.

While these plans and arrangements were yet immature, a circumstance occurred which threatened, for a time, wholly to defeat them. It seems that when Cleopatra's father first left Egypt, he had caused a report to be circulated there that he had been killed in the revolt. The object of this stratagem was to cover and conceal his flight. The government of Berenice soon discovered the truth, and learned that the fugitive had gone in the direction of Rome. They immediately inferred that he was going to appeal to the Roman people for aid, and they determined that, if that were the case, the Roman people, before deciding in his favor, should have the opportunity to hear their side of the story as well as his. They accordingly made preparations at once for sending a very imposing embassage to Rome. The deputation consisted of more than a hundred persons. The object of Berenice's government in sending so large a number was not only to evince their respect for the Roman people, and their sense of the magnitude of the question at issue, but also to guard against any efforts that Ptolemy might make to intercept the embassage on the way, or to buy off the members of it by bribes. The number, however large as it was, proved insufficient to accomplish this purpose. The whole Roman world was at this time in such a condition of disorder and violence, in the hands of the desperate and reckless military leaders who then bore sway, that there were everywhere abundant facilities for the commission of any conceivable crime. Ptolemy contrived, with the assistance of the fierce partisans who had espoused his cause, and who were deeply interested in his success on account of the rewards which were promised them, to waylay and destroy a large proportion of this company before they reached Rome. Some were assassinated; some were poisoned; some were tampered with and bought off by bribes. A small remnant reached Rome; but they were so intimidated by the dangers which surrounded them, that they did not dare to take any public action in respect to the business which had been committed to their charge. Ptolemy began to congratulate himself on having completely circumvented his daughter in her efforts to protect herself against his designs.

Instead of that, however, it soon proved that the effect of this atrocious treachery was exactly the contrary of what its perpetrators had expected. The knowledge of the facts became gradually extended among the people of Rome and it awakened a universal indignation. The party who had been originally opposed to Ptolemy's cause seized the opportunity to renew their opposition; and they gained so much strength from the general odium which Ptolemy's crimes had awakened, that Pompey found it almost impossible to sustain his cause.

At length the party opposed to Ptolemy found, or pretended to find, in certain sacred books, called the Sibylline Oracles, which were kept in the custody of the priests, and were supposed to contain prophetic intimations of the will of Heaven in respect to the conduct of public affairs, the following passage:

> "If a king of Egypt should apply to you for aid, treat him in a friendly manner, but do not furnish him with troops; for if you do, you will incur great danger."

This made new difficulty for Ptolemy's friends. They attempted, at first, to evade this inspired injunction by denying the reality of it. There was no such passage to be found, they said. It was all an invention of their enemies. This point seems to have been overruled, and then they attempted to give the passage some other than the obvious interpretation. Finally they maintained that, although it prohibited their furnishing Ptolemy himself with troops, it did not forbid their sending an armed force into Egypt under leaders of their own. *That* they could certainly do; and then, when the rebellion was suppressed, and Berenice's government overthrown, they could invite Ptolemy to return to his kingdom and resume his crown in a peaceful manner. This, they alleged, would not be "furnishing him with troops," and, of course would not be disobeying the oracle.

These attempts to evade the direction of the oracle on the part of Ptolemy's friends, only made the debates and dissensions between them and his enemies more violent than ever. Pompey made every effort in his power to aid Ptolemy's cause; but Lentulus, after long hesitation and delay, decided that it would not be safe for him to embark in it. At length, however, Gabinius, the lieutenant who commanded in Syria, was induced to undertake the enterprise. On certain promises which he received from Ptolemy, to be performed in case he succeeded, and with a certain encouragement, not very legal or regular, which Pompey gave him, in respect to the employment of the Roman troops under his command, he resolved to march to Egypt. His route, of course, would lie along the shores of the Mediterranean Sea, and through the desert, to Pelusium, which has already been mentioned as the frontier town on this side of Egypt. From Pelusium he was to march through the heart of the Delta to Alexandria, and, if successful in his invasion, overthrow the government of Berenice and Archelaus, and then, inviting Ptolemy to return, reinstate him on the throne.

In the prosecution of this dangerous enterprise, Gabinius relied strongly on the assistance of a very remarkable man, then his second in command, who afterward acted a very important part in the subsequent history of Cleopatra. His name was Mark Antony. Antony was born in Rome, of a very distinguished family, but his father died when he was very young, and being left subsequently much to himself, he became a very wild and dissolute young man. He wasted the property which his father had left him in folly and vice; and then going on desperately in the same career, he soon incurred enormous debts, and involved himself, in consequence, in inextricable difficulties. His creditors continually harassed him with importunities for money, and with suits at law to compel payments which he had no means of making. He was likewise incessantly pursued by the hostility of the many enemies that he had made in the city by his violence and his crimes. At length he absconded, and went to Greece.

Here Gabinius, when on his way to Syria, met him, and invited him to join his army rather than to remain where he was in idleness and destitution. Antony, who was as proud and lofty in spirit as he was degraded in morals and condition, refused to do this unless Gabinius would give him a command. Gabinius saw in the daring and reckless energy which Antony manifested the indications of the class of qualities which in those days made a successful soldier, and acceded to his terms. He gave him the command of his cavalry. Antony distinguished himself in the Syrian campaigns that followed, and was now full of eagerness to engage in this Egyptian enterprise. In fact, it was mainly his zeal and enthusiasm to embark in the undertaking which was the means of deciding Gabinius to consent to Ptolemy's proposals.

The danger and difficulty which they considered as most to be apprehended in the whole expedition was the getting across the desert to Pelusium. In fact, the great protection of Egypt had always been her isolation. The trackless and desolate sands, being wholly destitute of water, and utterly void, could be traversed, even by a caravan of peaceful travelers, only with great difficulty and danger. For an army to attempt to cross them, exposed, as the troops would necessarily be, to the assaults of enemies who might advance to meet them on the way, and sure of encountering a terrible opposition from fresh and vigorous bands when they should arrive—wayworn and exhausted by the physical hardships of the way—at the borders of the inhabited country, was a desperate undertaking. Many instances occurred in ancient times in which vast bodies of troops, in attempting marches over the deserts by which Egypt was surrounded, were wholly destroyed by famine or thirst, or overwhelmed by storms of sand.

These difficulties and dangers, however, did not at all intimidate Mark Antony. The anticipation, in fact, of the glory of surmounting them was one of the main inducements which led him to embark in the enterprise. The perils of the desert constituted one of the charms which made the expedition so attractive. He placed himself, therefore, at the head of his troop of cavalry, and set off across the sands in advance of Gabinius, to take Pelusium, in order thus to open a way for the main body of the army into Egypt. Ptolemy accompanied Antony. Gabinius was to follow.

With all his faults, to call them by no severer name, Mark Antony possessed certain great excellences of character. He was ardent, but then he was cool, collected, and sagacious; and there was a certain frank and manly generosity continually evincing itself in his conduct and character which made him a great favorite among his men. He was at this time about twenty-eight years old, of a tall and manly form, and of an expressive and intellectual cast of countenance. His forehead was high, his nose aquiline, and his eyes full of vivacity and life. He was accustomed to dress in a very plain and careless manner, and he assumed an air of the utmost familiarity and freedom in his intercourse with his soldiers. He would join them in their sports, joke with them, and good-naturedly receive their jokes in return; and take his meals, standing with them around their rude tables, in the open field. Such habits of intercourse with his men in a commander of ordinary character would have been fatal to his ascendency over them; but in Mark Antony's case, these frank and familiar manners seemed only to make the military genius and the intellectual power which he possessed the more conspicuous and the more universally admired.

Antony conducted his troop of horsemen across the desert in a very safe and speedy manner, and arrived before Pelusium. The city was not prepared to resist him. It surrendered at once, and the whole garrison fell into his hands as prisoners of war. Ptolemy demanded that they should all be immediately killed. They were rebels, he said, and, as such, ought to be put to death. Antony, however, as might have been expected from his character, absolutely refused to allow of any such barbarity. Ptolemy, since the power was not yet in his hands, was compelled to submit, and to postpone gratifying the spirit of vengeance which had so long been slumbering in his breast to a future day. He could the more patiently submit to this necessity, since it appeared that the day of his complete and final triumph over his daughter and all her adherents was now very nigh at hand.

In fact, Berenice and her government, when they heard of the arrival of Antony and Ptolemy at Pelusium, of the fall of that city, and of the approach of Gabinius with an overwhelming force of Roman soldiers, were struck with dismay. Archelaus, the husband of Berenice, had been, in former years, a personal friend of Antony's. Antony considered, in fact, that they were friends still, though required by what the historian calls their duty to fight each other for the possession of the kingdom. The government of Berenice raised an army. Archelaus took command of it, and advanced to meet the enemy. In the mean time, Gabinius arrived with the main body of the Roman troops, and commenced his march, in conjunction with Antony, toward the capital. As they were obliged to make a circuit to the southward, in order to avoid the inlets and lagoons which, on the northern coast of Egypt, penetrate for some distance into the land, their course led them through the heart of the Delta. Many battles were fought, the Romans every where gaining the victory. The Egyptian soldiers were, in fact, discontented and mutinous, perhaps, in part, because they considered the government on the side of which they were compelled to engage as, after all a usurpation. At length a great final battle was fought, which settled the controversy. Archelaus was slain upon the field, and Berenice was taken prisoner; their government was wholly overthrown, and the way was opened for the march of the Roman armies to Alexandria.

Mark Antony, when judged by our standards, was certainly, as well as Ptolemy, a depraved and vicious man; but his depravity was of a very different type from that of Cleopatra's father. The difference in the men, in one respect, was very clearly evinced by the objects toward which their interest and attention were respectively turned after this great battle. While the contest had been going on, the king and queen of Egypt, Archelaus and Berenice, were, of course, in the view both of Antony and Ptolemy, the two most conspicuous personages in the army of their enemies; and while Antony would naturally watch with the greatest interest the fate of his friend, the king, Ptolemy, would as naturally follow with the highest concern the destiny of his daughter. Accordingly, when the battle was over, while the mind of Ptolemy might, as we should naturally expect, be chiefly occupied by the fact that his *daughter* was made a captive, Antony's, we might suppose, would be engrossed by the tidings that his *friend* had been slain.

The one rejoiced and the other mourned. Antony sought for the body of his friend on the field of battle, and when it was found, he gave himself wholly to the work of providing for it a most magnificent burial. He seemed, at the funeral, to lament the death of his ancient comrade with real and unaffected grief. Ptolemy, on the other hand, was overwhelmed with joy at finding his daughter his captive. The long-wished-for hour for the gratification of his revenge had come at last, and the first use which he made of his power when he was put in possession of it at Alexandria was to order his daughter to be beheaded.

CHAPTER V.

ACCESSION TO THE THRONE.

Cleopatra.—Excitement in Alexandria.—Ptolemy restored.—Acquiescence of the people.—Festivities.—Popularity of Antony.—Antony's generosity.—Anecdote.—Antony and Cleopatra.—Antony returns to Rome.—Ptolemy's murders.—Pompey and Caesar.—Close of Ptolemy's reign.—Settlement of the succession.—Accession of Cleopatra.—She is married to her brother.—Pothinus, the eunuch.—His character and government.—Machinations of Pothinus.—Cleopatra is expelled. —Cleopatra's army.—Approaching contest. —Caesar and Pompey. —Battle of Pharsalia.—Pompey at Pelusium.—Treachery of Pothinus.—Caesar's pursuit of Pompey.—His danger.—Caesar at Alexandria.—Astonishment of the Egyptians.—Caesar presented with Pompey's head.—Pompey's seal.—Situation of Caesar.—His demands.—Conduct of Pothinus.—Quarrels—Policy of Pothinus. —Contentions.—Caesar sends to Syria for additional troops.

At the time when the unnatural quarrel between Cleopatra's father and her sister was working its way toward its dreadful termination, as related in the last chapter, she herself was residing at the royal palace in Alexandria, a blooming and beautiful girl of about fifteen. Fortunately for her, she was too young to take any active part personally in the contention. Her two brothers were still younger than herself. They all three remained, therefore, in the royal palaces, quiet spectators of the revolution, without being either benefited or injured by it. It is singular that the name of both the boys was Ptolemy.

The excitement in the city of Alexandria was intense and universal when the Roman army entered it to reinstate Cleopatra's father upon his throne. A very large portion of the inhabitants were pleased with having the former king restored. In fact, it appears, by a retrospect of the history of kings, that when a legitimate hereditary sovereign or dynasty is deposed and expelled by a rebellious population, no matter how intolerable may have been the tyranny, or how atrocious the crimes by which the patience of the subject was exhausted, the lapse of a very few years is ordinarily sufficient to produce a very general readiness to acquiesce in a restoration; and in this particular instance there had been no such superiority in the government of Berenice,

44

during the period while her power continued, over that of her father, which she had displaced, as to make this case an exception to the general rule. The mass of the people, therefore—all those, especially, who had taken no active part in Berenice's government—were ready to welcome Ptolemy back to his capital. Those who had taken such a part were all summarily executed by Ptolemy's orders.

There was, of course, a great excitement throughout the city on the arrival of the Roman army. All the foreign influence and power which had been exercised in Egypt thus far, and almost all the officers, whether civil or military, had been Greek. The coming of the Romans was the introduction of a new element of interest to add to the endless variety of excitements which animated the capital.

The restoration of Ptolemy was celebrated with games, spectacles, and festivities of every kind, and, of course, next to the king himself, the chief center of interest and attraction in all these public rejoicings would be the distinguished foreign generals by whose instrumentality the end had been gained.

Mark Antony was a special object of public regard and admiration at the time. His eccentric manners, his frank and honest air, his Roman simplicity of dress and demeanor, made him conspicuous; and his interposition to save the lives of the captured garrison of Pelusium, and the interest which he took in rendering such distinguished funeral honors to the enemy whom his army had slain in battle, impressed the people with the idea of a certain nobleness and magnanimity in his character, which, in spite of his faults, made him an object of general admiration and applause. The very faults of such a man assume often, in the eyes of the world, the guise and semblance of virtues. For example, it is related of Antony that, at one time in the course of his life, having a desire to make a present of some kind to a certain person, in requital for a favor which he had received from him, he ordered his treasurer to send a sum of money to his friend—and named for the sum to be sent an amount considerably greater than was really required under the circumstances of the case—acting thus, as he often did, under the influence of a blind and uncalculating generosity. The treasurer, more prudent than his master, wished to reduce the amount, but he did not dare directly to propose a reduction; so he counted out the money, and laid it in a pile in a place where Antony was to pass, thinking that when Antony saw the amount, he would perceive that it was too great. Antony, in passing by, asked what money that was. The treasurer said that it was the sum that he had ordered to be sent as a present to such a person, naming the individual intended. Antony was quick to perceive the object of the treasurer's maneuver. He immediately replied, "Ah! is that all? I thought the sum I named would make a better appearance than that; send him double the amount."

To determine, under such circumstances as these, to double an extravagance merely for the purpose of thwarting the honest attempt of a faithful servant to diminish it, made, too, in so cautious and delicate a way, is most certainly a fault. But it is one of those faults for which the world, in all ages, will persist in admiring and praising the perpetrator.

In a word, Antony became the object of general attention and favor during his continuance at Alexandria. Whether he particularly attracted Cleopatra's attention at this time or not does not appear. She, however, strongly attracted *his*. He admired her blooming beauty, her sprightliness and wit, and her various accomplishments. She was still, however, so young—being but fifteen years of age, while Antony was nearly thirty—that she probably made no very serious impression upon him. A short time after this, Antony went back to Rome, and did not see Cleopatra again for many years.

When the two Roman generals went away from Alexandria, they left a considerable portion of the army behind them, under Ptolemy's command, to aid him in keeping possession of his throne. Antony returned to Rome. He had acquired great renown by his march across the desert, and by the successful accomplishment of the invasion of Egypt and the restoration of Ptolemy. His funds, too, were replenished by the vast sums paid to him and to Gabinius by Ptolemy. The amount which Ptolemy is said to have agreed to pay as the price of his restoration was two thousand talents—equal to ten millions of dollars—a sum which shows on how great a scale the operations of this celebrated campaign were conducted. Ptolemy raised a large portion of the money required for his payments by confiscating the estates belonging to those friends of Berenice's government whom he ordered to be slain. It was said, in fact, that the numbers were very much increased of those that were condemned to die, by Ptolemy's standing in such urgent need of their property to meet his obligations.

Antony, through the results of this campaign, found himself suddenly raised from the position of a disgraced and homeless fugitive to that of one of the most wealthy and renowned, and, consequently, one of the most powerful personages in Rome. The great civil war broke out about this time between Caesar and Pompey. Antony espoused the cause of Caesar.

In the mean time, while the civil war between Caesar and Pompey was raging, Ptolemy succeeded in maintaining his seat on the throne, by the aid of the Roman soldiers whom Antony and Gabinius had left him, for about three years. When he found himself drawing toward the close of life, the question arose to his mind to whom he should leave his kingdom. Cleopatra was the oldest child, and she was a princess of great promise, both in respect to mental endowments and personal charms. Her brothers were considerably younger than she. The claim of a son, though younger, seemed to be naturally stronger than that of a daughter; but the commanding talents and rising influence of Cleopatra appeared to make it doubtful whether it would be safe to pass her by. The father settled the question in the way in which such difficulties were usually surmounted in the Ptolemy family. He ordained that Cleopatra should marry the oldest of her brothers, and that they two should jointly occupy the throne. Adhering also, still, to the idea of the alliance of Egypt with Rome, which had been the leading principle of the whole policy of his reign, he solemnly committed the execution of his will and the guardianship of his children, by a provision of the instrument itself, to the Roman Senate. The Senate accepted the appointment, and appointed Pompey as the agent, on their part, to perform the duties of the trust. The attention of Pompey was, immediately after that time, too much engrossed by the civil war waged between himself and Caesar, to take any active steps in respect to the duties of his appointment. It seemed, however, that none were necessary, for all parties in Alexandria appeared disposed, after the death of the king, to acquiesce in the arrangements which he had made, and to join in carrying them into effect. Cleopatra was married to her brother—yet, it is true, only a boy. He was about ten years old. She was herself about eighteen. They were both too young to govern; they could only reign. The affairs of the kingdom were, accordingly, conducted by two ministers whom their father had designated. These ministers were Pothinus, a eunuch, who was a sort of secretary of state, and Achillas, the commander-in-chief of the armies.

Thus, though Cleopatra, by these events, became nominally a queen, her real accession to the throne was not yet accomplished. There were still many difficulties and dangers to be passed through, before the period arrived when she became really a sovereign. She did not, herself, make any immediate attempt to hasten this period, but seems to have acquiesced, on the other hand, very quietly, for a time, in the arrangements which her father had made.

Pothinus was a eunuch. He had been, for a long time, an officer of government under Ptolemy, the father. He was a proud, ambitious, and domineering man, determined to rule, and very unscrupulous in respect to the means which he adopted to accomplish his ends. He had been accustomed to regard Cleopatra as a mere child. Now that she was queen, he was very unwilling that the real power should pass into her hands. The jealousy and ill will which he felt toward her increased rapidly as he found, in the course of to quiet and [illegible]ars after her father's death, that she was advancing rapidly in strength of character, and in the influence and ascendency which she was acquiring over all around her. Her beauty, her accomplishments, and a certain indescribable charm which pervaded all her demeanor, combined to give her great personal power. But, while these things awakened in other minds feelings of interest in Cleopatra and attachment to her, they only increased the jealousy and envy of Pothinus. Cleopatra was becoming his rival. He endeavored to thwart and circumvent her. He acted toward her in a haughty and overbearing manner, in order to keep her down to what he considered her proper place as his ward; for he was yet the guardian both of Cleopatra and her husband, and the regent of the realm.

Cleopatra had a great deal of what is sometimes called spirit, and her resentment was aroused by this treatment. Pothinus took pains to enlist her young husband, Ptolemy, on his side, as the quarrel advanced. Ptolemy was younger, and of a character much less marked and decided than Cleopatra. Pothinus saw that he could maintain control over him much more easily and for a much longer time than over Cleopatra. He contrived to awaken the young Ptolemy's jealousy of his wife's rising influence, and to induce him to join in efforts to thwart and counteract it. These attempts to turn her husband against her only aroused Cleopatra's resentment the more. Hers was not a spirit to be coerced. The palace was filled with the dissensions of the rivals. Pothinus and Ptolemy began to take measures for securing the army on their side. An open rupture finally ensued, and Cleopatra was expelled from the kingdom.

She went to Syria. Syria was the nearest place of refuge, and then, besides, it was the country from which the aid had been furnished by which her father had been restored to the throne when he had been expelled, in a similar manner, many years before. Her father, it is true, had gone first to Rome; but the succors which he had negotiated for had been sent from Syria. Cleopatra hoped to obtain the same assistance by going directly there.

Nor was she disappointed. She obtained an army, and commenced her march toward Egypt, following the same track which Antony and Gabinius had pursued in coming to reinstate her father. Pothinus raised an army and went forth to meet her. He took Achillas as the commander of the troops, and the young Ptolemy as the nominal sovereign; while he, as the young king's guardian and prime minister, exercised the real power. The troops of Pothinus advanced to Pelusium. Here they met the forces of Cleopatra coming from the east. The armies encamped not very far from each other, and both sides began to prepare for battle.

The battle, however, was not fought. It was prevented by the occurrence of certain great and unforeseen events which at this crisis suddenly burst upon the scene of Egyptian history, and turned the whole current of affairs into new and unexpected channels. The breaking out of the civil war between the great

Roman generals Caesar and Pompey, and their respective partisans, has already been mentioned as having occurred soon after the death of Cleopatra's father, and as having prevented Pompey from undertaking the office of executor of the will. This war had been raging ever since that time with terrible fury. Its distant thundering had been heard even in Egypt, but it was too remote to awaken there any special alarm. The immense armies of these two mighty conquerors had moved slowly—like two ferocious birds of prey, flying through the air, and fighting as they fly—across Italy into Greece, and from Greece, through Macedon, into Thessaly, contending in dreadful struggles with each other as they advanced, and trampling down and destroying every thing in their way. At length a great final battle had been fought at Pharsalia. Pompey had been totally defeated. He had fled to the sea-shore, and there, with a few ships and a small number of followers, he had pushed out upon the Mediterranean, not knowing whither to fly, and overwhelmed with wretchedness and despair. Caesar followed him in eager pursuit. He had a small fleet of galleys with him, on board of which he had embarked two or three thousand men. This was a force suitable, perhaps, for the pursuit of a fugitive, but wholly insufficient for any other design.

Pompey thought of Ptolemy. He remembered the efforts which he himself had made for the cause of Ptolemy Auletes, at Rome, and the success of those efforts in securing that monarch's restoration—an event through which alone the young Ptolemy had been enabled to attain the crown. He came, therefore, to Pelusium, and, anchoring his little fleet off the shore, sent to the land to ask Ptolemy to receive and protect him. Pothinus, who was really the commander in Ptolemy's army, made answer to this application that Pompey should be received and protected, and that he would send out a boat to bring him to the shore. Pompey felt some misgivings in respect to this proffered hospitality, but he finally concluded to go to the shore in the boat which Pothinus sent for him. As soon as he landed, the Egyptians, by Pothinus's orders, stabbed and beheaded him on the sand. Pothinus and his council had decided that this would be the safest course. If they were to receive Pompey, they reasoned, Caesar would be made their enemy; if they refused to receive him, Pompey himself would be offended, and they did not know which of the two it would be safe to displease; for they did not know in what way, if both the generals were to be allowed to live, the war would ultimately end. "But by killing Pompey," they said, "we shall be sure to please Caesar and Pompey himself will *lie still.*"

In the mean time, Caesar, not knowing to what part of Egypt Pompey had fled, pressed on directly to Alexandria. He exposed himself to great danger in so doing, for the forces under his command were not sufficient to protect him in case of his becoming involved in difficulties with the authorities there. Nor could he, when once arrived on the Egyptian coast, easily go away again; for, at the season of the year in which these events occurred, there was a periodical wind which blew steadily toward that part of the coast, and, while it made it very easy for a fleet of ships to go to Alexandria, rendered it almost impossible for them to return.

Caesar was very little accustomed to shrink from danger in any of his enterprises and plans, though still he was usually prudent and circumspect. In this instance, however, his ardent interest in the pursuit of Pompey overruled all considerations of personal safety. He arrived at Alexandria, but he found that Pompey was not there. He anchored his vessels in the port, landed his troops, and established himself in the city. These two events, the assassination of one of the great Roman generals on the eastern extremity of the coast, and the arrival of the other, at the same moment, at Alexandria, on the western, burst suddenly upon Egypt together, like simultaneous claps of thunder. The tidings struck the whole country with astonishment, and immediately engrossed universal attention. At the camps both of Cleopatra and Ptolemy, at Pelusium, all was excitement and wonder. Instead of thinking of a battle, both parties were wholly occupied in speculating on the results which were likely to accrue, to one side or to the other, under the totally new and unexpected aspect which public affairs had assumed.

Of course the thoughts of all were turned toward Alexandria. Pothinus immediately proceeded to the city, taking with him the young king. Achillas, too, either accompanied them, or followed soon afterward. They carried with them the head of Pompey, which they had cut off on the shore where they had killed him, and also a seal which they took from his finger. When they arrived at Alexandria, they sent the head, wrapped up in a cloth, and also the seal, as presents to Caesar. Accustomed as they were to the brutal deeds and heartless cruelties of the Ptolemies, they supposed that Caesar would exult at the spectacle of the dissevered and ghastly head of his great rival and enemy. Instead of this, he was shocked and displeased, and ordered the head to be buried with the most solemn and imposing funeral ceremonies. He, however, accepted and kept the seal. The device engraved upon it was a lion holding a sword in his paw—a fit emblem of the characters of the men, who, though in many respects magnanimous and just, had filled the whole world with the terror of their quarrels.

The army of Ptolemy, while he himself and his immediate counselors went to Alexandria, was left at Pelusium, under the command of other officers, to watch Cleopatra. Cleopatra herself would have been pleased, also, to repair to Alexandria and appeal to Caesar, if it had been in her power to do so; but she was beyond the confines of the country, with a powerful army of her enemies ready to intercept her on any attempt to enter or pass through it. She remained, therefore, at Pelusium, uncertain what to do.

In the mean time, Caesar soon found himself in a somewhat embarrassing situation at Alexandria. He had been accustomed, for many years, to the possession and the exercise of the most absolute and despotic power, wherever he might be; and now that Pompey, his great rival, was dead, he considered himself the monarch and master of the world. He had not, however, at Alexandria, any means sufficient to maintain and enforce such pretensions, and yet he was not of a spirit to abate, on that account, in the slightest degree, the advancing of them. He established himself in the palaces of Alexandria as if he were himself the king. He moved, in state, through the streets of the city, at the head of his guards, and displaying the customary emblems of supreme authority used at Rome. He claimed the six thousand talents which Ptolemy Auletes had formerly promised him for procuring a treaty of alliance with Rome, and he called upon Pothinus to pay the balance due. He said, moreover, that by the will of Auletes the Roman people had been made the executor; and that it devolved upon him as the Roman consul, and, consequently, the representative of the Roman people, to assume that trust, and in the discharge of it to settle the dispute between Ptolemy and Cleopatra, and he called upon Ptolemy to prepare and lay before him a statement of his claims, and the grounds on which he maintained his right to the throne to the exclusion of Cleopatra.

On the other hand, Pothinus, who had been as little accustomed to acknowledge a superior as Caesar, though his supremacy and domination had been exercised on a somewhat humbler scale, was obstinate and pertinacious in resisting all these demands, though the means and methods which he resorted to were of a character corresponding to his weak and ignoble mind. He fomented quarrels in the streets between the Alexandrian populace and Caesar's soldiers. He thought that, as the number of troops under Caesar's command in the city, and of vessels in the port, was small, he could tease and worry the Romans with impunity, though he had not the courage openly to attack them. He pretended to be a friend, or, at least, not an enemy, and yet he conducted himself toward them in an overbearing and insolent manner. He had agreed to make arrangements for supplying them with food, and he did this by procuring damaged provisions of a most wretched quality; and when the soldiers remonstrated, he said to them, that they who lived at other people's cost had no right to complain of their fare. He caused wooden and earthen vessels to be used in the palace, and said, in explanation, that he had been compelled to sell all the gold and silver plate of the royal household to meet the exactions of Caesar. He busied himself, too, about the city, in endeavoring to excite odium against Caesar's proposal to hear and decide the question at issue between Cleopatra and Ptolemy. Ptolemy was a sovereign, he said, and was not amenable to any foreign power whatever. Thus, without the courage or the energy to attempt any open, manly, and effectual system of hostility, he contented himself with making all the difficulty in his power, by urging an incessant pressure of petty, vexatious, and provoking, but useless annoyances. Caesar's demands may have been unjust, but they were bold, manly, and undisguised. The eunuch may have been right in resisting them; but the mode was so mean and contemptible, that mankind have always taken part with Caesar in the sentiments which they have formed as spectators of the contest.

With the very small force which Caesar had at his command, and shut up as he was in the midst of a very great and powerful city, in which both the garrison and the population were growing more and more hostile to him every day, he soon found his situation was beginning to be attended with very serious danger. He could not retire from the scene. He probably would not have retired if he could have done so. He remained, therefore, in the city, conducting himself all the time with prudence and circumspection, but yet maintaining, as at first, the same air of confident self-possession and superiority which always characterized his demeanor. He, however, dispatched a messenger forthwith into Syria, the nearest country under the Roman sway, with orders that several legions which were posted there should be embarked and forwarded to Alexandria with the utmost possible celerity.

CHAPTER VI.

CLEOPATRA AND Caesar.

Cleopatra's perplexity.—She resolves To go to Alexandria.—Cleopatra's message to Caesar.—Caesar's reply.—Apollodorus's stratagem.—Cleopatra and Caesar—First impressions.—Caesar's attachment.—Caesar's wife.—His fondness for Cleopatra.—Cleopatra's foes.—She commits her cause to Caesar.—Caesar's pretensions.—He sends for Ptolemy.—Ptolemy's indignation.—His complaints against Caesar.—Great tumult in the city.— Excitement of the populace.—Caesar's forces—Ptolemy made prisoner.— Caesar's address to the people.—Its effects.—The mob dispersed.—Caesar convenes an assembly.—Caesar's decision. —Satisfaction of the assembly.— Festivals and rejoicings. —Pothinus and Achillas.—Plot of Pothinus and Achillas.—Escape of Achillas.—March of the Egyptian army.—Measures of Caesar. —Murder of the messengers.—Intentions of Achillas—Cold-blooded assassination.—Advance of Achillas—Caesar's arrangements for defense.— Cleopatra and Ptolemy.—Double dealing of Pothinus.—He is detected.—

Pothinus beheaded—Arsinoe and Ganymede—Flight of Arsinoe—She is proclaimed queen by the army.—Perplexity of the young Ptolemy.

In the mean time, while the events related in the last chapter were taking place at Alexandria, Cleopatra remained anxious and uneasy in her camp, quite uncertain, for a time, what it was best for her to do. She wished to be at Alexandria. She knew very well that Caesar's power in controlling the course of affairs in Egypt would necessarily be supreme. She was, of course, very earnest in her desire to be able to present her cause before him. As it was, Ptolemy and Pothinus were in communication with the arbiter, and, for aught she knew, assiduously cultivating his favor, while she was far away, her cause unheard, her wrongs unknown, and perhaps even her existence forgotten. Of course, under such circumstances, she was very earnest to get to Alexandria.

But how to accomplish this purpose was a source of great perplexity. She could not march thither at the head of an army, for the army of the king was strongly intrenched at Pelusium, and effectually barred the way. She could not attempt to pass alone, or with few attendants, through the country, for every town and village was occupied with garrisons and officers under the orders of Pothinus, and she would be certainly intercepted. She had no fleet, and could not, therefore, make the passage by sea. Besides, even if she could by any means reach the gates of Alexandria, how was she to pass safely through the streets of the city to the palace where Caesar resided, since the city, except in Caesar's quarters, was wholly in the hands of Pothinus's government? The difficulties in the way of accomplishing her object seemed thus almost insurmountable.

She was, however, resolved to make the attempt. She sent a message to Caesar, asking permission to appear before him and plead her own cause. Caesar replied, urging her by all means to come. She took a single boat, and with the smallest number of attendants possible, made her way along the coast to Alexandria. The man on whom she principally relied in this hazardous expedition was a domestic named Apollodorus. She had, however, some other attendants besides. When the party reached Alexandria, they waited until night, and then advanced to the foot of the walls of the citadel. Here Apollodorus rolled the queen up in a piece of carpeting, and, covering the whole package with a cloth, he tied it with a thong, so as to give it the appearance of a bale of ordinary merchandise, and then throwing the load across his shoulder, he advanced into the city. Cleopatra was at this time about twenty-one years of age, but she was of a slender and graceful form, and the burden was, consequently, not very heavy. Apollodorus came to the gates of the palace where Caesar was residing. The guards at the gates asked him what it was that he was carrying. He said that it was a present for Caesar. So they allowed him to pass, and the pretended porter carried his package safely in.

When it was unrolled, and Cleopatra came out to view, Caesar was perfectly charmed with the spectacle. In fact, the various conflicting emotions which she could not but feel under such circumstances as these, imparted a double interest to her beautiful and expressive face, and to her naturally bewitching manners. She was excited by the adventure through which she had passed, and yet pleased with her narrow escape from its dangers. The curiosity and interest which she felt on the one hand, in respect to the great personage into whose presence she had been thus strangely ushered, was very strong; but then, on the other hand, it was chastened and subdued by that feeling of timidity which, in new and unexpected situations like these, and under a consciousness of being the object of eager observation to the other sex, is inseparable from the nature of woman.

The conversation which Caesar held with Cleopatra deepened the impression which her first appearance had made upon him. Her intelligence and animation, the originality of her ideas, and the point and pertinency of her mode of expressing them, made her, independently of her personal charms, an exceedingly entertaining and agreeable companion. She, in fact, completely won the great conqueror's heart; and, through the strong attachment to her which he immediately formed, he became wholly disqualified to act impartially between her and her brother in regard to their respective rights to the crown. We call Ptolemy Cleopatra's brother; for, though he was also, in fact, her husband, still, as he was only ten or twelve years of age at the time of Cleopatra's expulsion from Alexandria, the marriage had been probably regarded, thus far, only as a mere matter of form. Caesar was now about fifty-two. He had a wife, named Calpurnia, to whom he had been married about ten years. She was living, at this time, in an unostentatious and quiet manner at Rome. She was a lady of an amiable and gentle character, devotedly attached to her husband, patient and forbearing in respect to his faults, and often anxious and unhappy at the thought of the difficulties and dangers in which his ardent and unbounded ambition so often involved him.

Caesar immediately began to take a very strong interest in Cleopatra's cause. He treated her personally with the fondest attention, and it was impossible for her not to reciprocate in some degree the kind feeling with which he regarded her. It was, in fact, something altogether new to her to have a warm and devoted friend, espousing her cause, tendering her protection, and seeking in every way to promote her happiness. Her father had all his life neglected her. Her brother, of years and understanding totally inferior to hers, whom she had been compelled to make her husband, had become her mortal enemy. It is true that, in depriving her of her inheritance and expelling her from her native land, he had been only the tool and instrument of more designing men. This, however, far from improving the point of view from which she regarded him, made him appear not only hateful, but contemptible too. All the officers of government, also, in the Alexandrian court had turned against her, because they had supposed that they could control her brother more easily if she were away. Thus she had always been surrounded by selfish, mercenary, and implacable foes. Now, for the first time, she seemed to have a friend. A protector had suddenly arisen to support and defend her,—a man of very alluring person and manners, of a very noble and generous spirit, and of the very highest station. He loved her, and she could not refrain from loving him in return. She committed her cause entirely into his hands, confided to him all her interests, and gave herself up wholly into his power.

Nor was the unbounded confidence which she reposed in him undeserved, so far as related to his efforts to restore her to her throne. The legions which Caesar had sent for into Syria had not yet arrived, and his situation in Alexandria was still very defenseless and very precarious. He did not, however, on this account, abate in the least degree the loftiness and self confidence of the position which he had assumed, but he commenced immediately the work of securing Cleopatra's restoration. This quiet assumption of the right and power to arbitrate and decide such a question as that of the claim to the throne, in a country where he had accidentally landed and found rival claimants disputing for the succession, while he was still wholly destitute of the means of enforcing the superiority which he so coolly assumed, marks the immense ascendency which the Roman power had attained at this time in the estimation of mankind, and is, besides, specially characteristic of the genius and disposition of Caesar.

Very soon after Cleopatra had come to him, Caesar sent for the young Ptolemy, and urged upon him the duty and expediency of restoring Cleopatra. Ptolemy was beginning now to attain an age at which he might be supposed to have some opinion of his own on such a question. He declared himself utterly opposed to any such design. In the course of the conversation he learned that Cleopatra had arrived at Alexandria, and that she was then concealed in Caesar's palace. This intelligence awakened in his mind the greatest excitement and indignation. He went away from Caesar's presence in a rage. He tore the diadem which he was accustomed to wear in the streets, from his head, threw it down, and trampled it under his feet. He declared to the people that he was betrayed, and displayed the most violent indications of vexation and chagrin. The chief subject of his complaint, in the attempts which he made to awaken the popular indignation against Caesar and the Romans, was the disgraceful impropriety of the position which his sister had assumed in surrendering herself as she had done to Caesar. It is most probable, however, unless his character was very different from that of every other Ptolemy in the line, that what really awakened his jealousy and anger was fear of the commanding influence and power to which Cleopatra was likely to attain through the agency of so distinguished a protector, rather than any other consequences of his friendship, or any real considerations of delicacy in respect to his sister's good name or his own marital honor.

However this may be, Ptolemy, together with Pothinus and Achillas, and all his other friends and adherents, who joined him in the terrible outcry that he made against the coalition which he had discovered between Cleopatra and Caesar, succeeded in producing a very general and violent tumult throughout the city. The populace were aroused, and began to assemble in great crowds, and full of indignation and anger. Some knew the facts, and acted under something like an understanding of the cause of their anger. Others only knew that the aim of this sudden outbreak was to assault the Romans, and were ready, on any pretext, known or unknown, to join in any deeds of violence directed against these foreign intruders. There were others still, and these, probably, far the larger portion, who knew nothing and understood nothing but that there was to be tumult and a riot in and around the palaces, and were, accordingly, eager to be there.

Ptolemy and his officers had no large body of troops in Alexandria; for the events which had thus far occurred since Caesar's arrival had succeeded each other so rapidly, that a very short time had yet elapsed, and the main army remained still at Pelusium. The main force, therefore, by which Caesar was now attacked, consisted of the population of the city, headed, perhaps, by the few guards which the young king had at his command.

Caesar, on his part, had but a small portion of his forces at the palace where he was attacked. The rest were scattered about the city. He, however, seems to have felt no alarm. He did not even confine himself to acting on the defensive. He sent out a detachment of his soldiers with orders to seize Ptolemy and bring him in a prisoner. Soldiers trained, disciplined, and armed as the Roman veterans were, and nerved by the ardor and enthusiasm which seemed always to animate troops which were under Caesar's personal command, could accomplish almost any undertaking against a mere populace, however numerous or however furiously excited they might be. The soldiers sallied out, seized Ptolemy, and brought him in.

The populace were at first astounded at the daring presumption of this deed, and then exasperated at the indignity of it, considered as a violation of the person of their sovereign. The tumult would have greatly increased, had it not been that Caesar,—who had now attained all his ends in thus having brought Cleopatra and Ptolemy both within his power,—thought it most expedient to allay it. He accordingly ascended to the window of a tower, or of some other elevated portion of his palace, so high that missiles from the mob below could not reach him, and began to make signals expressive of his wish to address them.

When silence was obtained, he made them a speech well calculated to quiet the excitement. He told them that he did not pretend to any right to judge between Cleopatra and Ptolemy as their superior, but only in the performance of the duty solemnly assigned by Ptolemy Auletes, the father, to the Roman people, whose representative he was. Other than this he claimed no jurisdiction in the case; and his only wish, in the discharge of the duty which devolved upon him to consider the cause, was to settle the question in a manner just and equitable to all the parties concerned, and thus arrest the progress of the civil war, which, if not arrested, threatened to involve the country in the most terrible calamities. He counseled them, therefore, to disperse, and no longer disturb the peace of the city. He would immediately take measures for trying the question between Cleopatra and Ptolemy, and he did not doubt but that they would all be satisfied with his decision.

This speech, made, as it was, in the eloquent and persuasive, and yet dignified and imposing manner for which Caesar's harangues to turbulent assemblies like these were so famed, produced a great effect. Some were convinced, others were silenced; and those whose resentment and anger were not appeased, found themselves deprived of their power by the pacification of the rest. The mob was dispersed, and Ptolemy remained with Cleopatra in Caesar's custody.

The next day, Caesar, according to his promise, convened an assembly of the principal people of Alexandria and officers of state, and then brought out Ptolemy and Cleopatra, that he might decide their cause. The original will which Ptolemy Auletes had executed had been deposited in the public archives of Alexandria, and carefully preserved there. An authentic copy of it had been sent to Rome. Caesar caused the original will to be brought out and read to the assembly. The provisions of it were perfectly explicit and clear. It required that Cleopatra and Ptolemy should be married, and then settled the sovereign power upon them jointly, as king and queen. It recognized the Roman commonwealth as the ally of Egypt, and constituted the Roman government the executor of the will, and the guardian of the king and queen. In fact, so clear and explicit was this document, that the simple reading of it seemed to be of itself a decision of the question. When, therefore, Caesar announced that, in his judgment, Cleopatra was entitled to share the supreme power with Ptolemy, and that it was his duty, as the representative of the Roman power and the executor of the will, to protect both the king and the queen in their respective rights, there seemed to be nothing that could be said against his decision.

Besides Cleopatra and Ptolemy, there were two other children of Ptolemy Auletes in the royal family at this time. One was a girl, named Arsinoe. The other, a boy, was, singularly enough, named, like his brother, Ptolemy. These children were quite young, but Caesar thought that it would perhaps gratify the Alexandrians, and lead them to acquiesce more readily in his decision, if he were to make some royal provision for them. He accordingly proposed to assign the island of Cyprus as a realm for them. This was literally a gift, for Cyprus was at this time a Roman possession.

The whole assembly seemed satisfied with this decision except Pothinus. He had been so determined and inveterate an enemy to Cleopatra, that, as he was well aware, her restoration must end in his downfall and ruin. He went away from the assembly moodily determining that he would not submit to the decision, but would immediately adopt efficient measures to prevent its being carried into effect.

Caesar made arrangements for a series of festivals and celebrations, to commemorate and confirm the reestablishment of a good understanding between the king and the queen, and the consequent termination of the war. Such celebrations, he judged, would have great influence in removing any remaining animosities from the minds of the people, and restore the dominion of a kind and friendly feeling throughout the city.

The people fell in with these measures, and cordially co-operated to give them effect; but Pothinus and Achillas, though they suppressed all outward expressions of discontent, made incessant efforts in secret to organize a party, and to form plans for overthrowing the influence of Caesar, and making Ptolemy again the sole and exclusive sovereign.

Pothinus represented to all whom he could induce to listen to him that Caesar's real design was to make Cleopatra queen alone, and to depose Ptolemy, and urged them to combine with him to resist a policy which would end in bringing Egypt under the dominion of a woman. He also formed a plan, in connection with Achillas, for ordering the army back from Pelusium. The army consisted of thirty thousand men. If that army could be brought to Alexandria and kept under Pothinus's orders, Caesar and his three thousand Roman soldiers would be, they thought, wholly at their mercy.

There was, however, one danger to be guarded against in ordering the army to march toward the capital, and that was, that Ptolemy, while under Caesar's influence, might open communication with the officers, and so obtain command of its movements, and thwart all the conspirators' designs. To prevent this, it was arranged between Pothinus and Achillas that the latter should make his escape from Alexandria, proceed immediately to the camp at Pelusium, resume the command of the troops there, and conduct them himself to the capital; and that in all these operations, and also subsequently on his arrival, he should obey no orders unless they came to him through Pothinus himself.

Although sentinels and guards were probably stationed at the gates and avenues leading from the city Achillas contrived to effect his escape and to join the army. He placed himself at the head of the forces, and commenced his march toward the capital. Pothinus remained all the time within the city as a spy, pretending to acquiesce in Caesar's decision, and to be on friendly terms with him, but really plotting for his overthrow, and obtaining all the information which his position enabled him to command, in order that he might co-operate with the army and Achillas when they should arrive.

All these things were done with the utmost secrecy, and so cunning and adroit were the conspirators in forming and executing their plots, that Caesar seems to have had no knowledge of the measures which his enemies were taking, until he suddenly heard that the main body of Ptolemy's army was approaching the city, at least twenty thousand strong. In the mean time, however, the forces which he had sent for from Syria had not arrived, and no alternative was left but to defend the capital and himself as well as he could with the very small force which he had at his disposal.

He determined, however, first, to try the effect of orders sent out in Ptolemy's name to forbid the approach of the army to the city. Two officers were accordingly intrusted with these orders, and sent out to communicate them to Achillas. The names of these officers were Dioscorides and Serapion.

It shows in a very striking point of view to what an incredible exaltation the authority and consequence of a sovereign king rose in those ancient days, in the minds of men, that Achillas, at the moment when these men made their appearance in the camp, bearing evidently some command from Ptolemy in the city, considered it more prudent to kill them at once, without hearing their message, rather than to allow the orders to be delivered and then take the responsibility of disobeying them. If he could succeed in marching to Alexandria and in taking possession of the city, and then in expelling Caesar and Cleopatra and restoring Ptolemy to the exclusive possession of the throne, he knew very well that the king would rejoice in the result, and would overlook all irregularities on his part in the means by which he had accomplished it, short of absolute disobedience of a known command. Whatever might be the commands that these messengers were bringing him, he supposed that they doubtless originated, not in Ptolemy's own free will, but that they were dictated by the authority of Caesar. Still, they would be commands coming in Ptolemy's name, and the universal experience of officers serving under the military despots of those ancient days showed that, rather than to take the responsibility of directly disobeying a royal order once received, it was safer to avoid receiving it by murdering the messengers.

Achillas therefore directed the officers to be seized and slain. They were accordingly taken off and speared by the soldiers, and then the bodies were borne away. The soldiers, however, it was found, had not done their work effectually. There was no interest for them in such a cold-blooded assassination, and perhaps something like a sentiment of compassion restrained their hands. At any rate, though both the men were desperately wounded, one only died. The other lived and recovered.

Achillas continued to advance toward the city. Caesar, finding that the crisis which was approaching was becoming very serious in its character, took, himself, the whole command within the capital, and began to make the best arrangements possible under the circumstances of the case to defend himself there. His numbers were altogether too small to defend the whole city against the overwhelming force which was advancing to assail it. He accordingly intrenched his troops in the palaces and in the citadel, and in such other parts of the city as it seemed practicable to defend. He barricaded all the streets and avenues leading to these points, and fortified the gates. Nor did he, while thus doing all in his power to employ the insufficient means of defense already in his hands to the best advantage, neglect the proper exertions for obtaining succor from abroad. He sent off galleys to Syria, to Cyprus, to Rhodes, and to every other point accessible from Alexandria where Roman troops might be expected to be found, urging the authorities there to forward re-enforcements to him with the utmost possible dispatch.

During all this time Cleopatra and Ptolemy remained in the palace with Caesar, both ostensibly co-operating with him in his councils and measures for defending the city from Achillas. Cleopatra, of course, was sincere and in earnest in this co-operation; but Ptolemy's adhesion to the common cause was very little to be relied upon. Although, situated as he was, he was compelled to seem to be on Caesar's side, he must have secretly desired that Achillas should succeed and Caesar's plans be overthrown. Pothinus was more active, though not less cautious in his hostility to them. He opened secret communication with Achillas, sending him information, from time to time, of what took place within the walls, and of the arrangements made there for the defense of the city against him, and gave him also directions how to proceed. He was very wary and sagacious in all these movements, feigning all the time to be on Caesar's side. He pretended to be very zealously employed in aiding Caesar to secure more effectually the various points where attacks were to be expected, and in maturing and completing the arrangements for defense.

But, notwithstanding all his cunning, he was detected in his double dealing, and his career was suddenly brought to a close, before the great final conflict came on. There was a barber in Caesar's household, who, for some cause or other, began to suspect Pothinus; and, having little else to do, he employed himself in watching the eunuch's movements and reporting them to Caesar. Caesar directed the barber to continue his observations. He did so; his suspicions were soon confirmed, and at length a letter, which Pothinus had written to Achillas, was intercepted and brought to Caesar. This furnished the necessary proof of what they called his guilt, and Caesar ordered him to be beheaded.

This circumstance produced, of course, a great excitement within the palace, for Pothinus had been for many years the great ruling minister of state,—the king, in fact, in all but in name. His execution alarmed a great many others, who, though in Caesar's power, were secretly wishing that Achillas might prevail. Among those most disturbed by these fears was a man named Ganymede. He was the officer who had charge of Arsinoe, Cleopatra's sister. The arrangement which Caesar had proposed for establishing her in conjunction with her brother Ptolemy over the island of Cyprus had not gone into effect; for, immediately after the decision of Caesar, the attention of all concerned had been wholly engrossed by the tidings of the advance of the army, and by the busy preparations which were required on all hands for the impending contest. Arsinoe, therefore, with her governor Ganymede, remained in the palace. Ganymede had joined Pothinus in his plots; and when Pothinus was beheaded, he concluded that it would be safest for him to fly.

He accordingly resolved to make his escape from the city, taking Arsinoe with him. It was a very hazardous attempt but he succeeded in accomplishing it. Arsinoe was very willing to go, for she was now beginning to be old enough to feel the impulse of that insatiable and reckless ambition which seemed to form such an essential element in the character of every son and daughter in the whole Ptolemaic line. She was insignificant and powerless where she was, but at the head of the army she might become immediately a queen.

It resulted, in the first instance, as she had anticipated. Achillas and his army received her with acclamations. Under Ganymede's influence they decided that, as all the other members of the royal family were in durance, being held captive by a foreign general, who had by chance obtained possession of the capital, and were thus incapacitated for exercising the royal power, the crown devolved upon Arsinoe; and they accordingly proclaimed her queen.

Every thing was now prepared for a desperate and determined contest for the crown between Cleopatra, with Caesar for her minister and general, on the one side, and Arsinoe, with Ganymede and Achillas for her chief officers, on the other. The young Ptolemy, in the mean time, remained Caesar's prisoner, confused with the intricacies in which the quarrel had become involved, and scarcely knowing now what to wish in respect to the issue of the contest. It was very difficult to foresee whether it would be best for him that Cleopatra or that Arsinoe should succeed.

CHAPTER VII.

THE ALEXANDRINE WAR.

The Alexandrine war.—Forces of Caesar.—The Egyptian army.—Fugitive slaves.—Dangerous situation of Caesar.—Presence of Caesar.—Influence of Cleopatra.—First measures of Caesar.—Caesar's stores.—Military engines.—The mole.—View of Alexandria.—Necessity of taking possession of the mole.—Egyptian fleet.—Caesar burns the shipping.—The fort taken.—Burning of Alexandria.—Achillas beheaded.—Plans of Ganymede.—His vigorous measures.—Messengers of Ganymede.—Their instructions.—Ganymede cuts off Caesar's supply of water.—Panic of the soldiers.—Caesar's wells.—Arrival of the transports.—The transports in distress.—Lowness of the coast.—A combat.—Caesar successful. —Ganymede equips a fleet.—A naval conflict.—Caesar in danger. —Another victory.—The Egyptians discouraged.—Secret messengers. —Dissimulation of Ptolemy—Arrival of Mithradates.—Defeat of Ptolemy. —Terror and confusion.—Death of Ptolemy.—Cleopatra queen.—General disapprobation of Caesar's course. —Cleopatra's son Caesarion.—Public opinion of her conduct.—Caesar departs for Rome.—He takes Arsinoe with him.

The war which ensued as the result of the intrigues and maneuvers described in the last chapter is known in the history of Rome and Julius Caesar as the Alexandrine war. The events which occurred during the progress of it, and its termination at last in the triumph of Caesar and Cleopatra, will form the subject of this chapter.

Achillas had greatly the advantage over Caesar at the outset of the contest, in respect to the strength of the forces under his command. Caesar, in fact, had with him only a detachment of three or four thousand men, a small body of troops which he had hastily put on board a little squadron of Rhodian galleys for pursuing Pompey across the Mediterranean. When he set sail from the European shores with this inconsiderable fleet, it is probable that he had no expectation even of landing in Egypt at all, and much less of being involved in great military undertakings there. Achillas, on the other hand, was at the head of a force of twenty thousand effective men. His troops were, it is true, of a somewhat miscellaneous character, but they were all veteran soldiers, inured to the climate of Egypt, and skilled in all the modes of warfare which were suited to the character of the country. Some of them were Roman soldiers, men who had come with the army of Mark Antony from Syria when Ptolemy Auletes, Cleopatra's father, was reinstated on the throne, and had been left in Egypt, in Ptolemy's service, when Antony returned to Rome. Some were native Egyptians. There was also in the army of Achillas a large number of fugitive slaves,—refugees who had made their escape from various points along the shores of the Mediterranean, at different periods, and had been from time to time incorporated into the Egyptian army. These fugitives were all men of the most determined and desperate character.

Achillas had also in his command a force of two thousand horse. Such a body of cavalry made him, of course, perfect master of all the open country outside the city walls. At the head of these troops Achillas gradually advanced to the very gates of Alexandria, invested the city on every side, and shut Caesar closely in.

The danger of the situation in which Caesar was placed was extreme; but he had been so accustomed to succeed in extricating himself from the most imminent perils, that neither he himself nor his army seem to have experienced any concern in respect to the result. Caesar personally felt a special pride and pleasure in encountering the difficulties and dangers which now beset him, because Cleopatra was with him to witness his demeanor, to admire his energy and courage, and to reward by her love the efforts and sacrifices which he was making in espousing her cause. She confided every thing to him, but she watched all the proceedings with the most eager interest, elated with hope in respect to the result, and proud of the champion who had thus volunteered to defend her. In a word, her heart was full of gratitude, admiration, and love.

The immediate effect, too, of the emotions which she felt so strongly was greatly to heighten her natural charms. The native force and energy of her character were softened and subdued. Her voice, which always possessed a certain inexpressible charm, was endued with new sweetness through the influence of affection. Her countenance beamed with fresh animation and beauty, and the sprightliness and vivacity of her character, which became at later periods of her life boldness and eccentricity, now being softened and restrained within proper limits by the respectful regard with which she looked upon Caesar, made her an enchanting companion. Caesar was, in fact, entirely intoxicated with the fascinations which she unconsciously displayed.

Under other circumstances than these, a personal attachment so strong, formed by a military commander while engaged in active service, might have been expected to interfere in some degree with the discharge of his duties; but in this case, since it was for Cleopatra's sake and in her behalf that the operations which Caesar had undertaken were to be prosecuted, his love for her only stimulated the spirit and energy with which he engaged in them.

The first measure to be adopted was, as Caesar plainly perceived, to concentrate and strengthen his position in the city, so that he might be able to defend himself there against Achillas until he should receive re-enforcements from abroad. For this purpose he selected a certain group of palaces and citadels which lay together near the head of the long pier or cause way which led to the Pharos, and, withdrawing his troops from all other parts of the city, established them there. The quarter which he thus occupied contained the great city arsenals and public granaries. Caesar brought together all the arms and munitions of war which he could find in other parts of the city, and also all the corn and other provisions which were contained either in the public depots or in private warehouses, and stored the whole within his lines. He then inclosed the whole quarter with strong defenses. The avenues leading to it were barricaded with walls of stone. Houses in the vicinity, which might have afforded shelter to an enemy, were demolished and the materials used in constructing walls wherever they were needed, or in strengthening the barricades. Prodigious military engines, made to throw heavy stones, and beams of wood, and other ponderous missiles, were set up within his lines, and openings were made in the walls and other defenses of the citadel, wherever necessary, to facilitate the action of these machines.

There was a strong fortress situated at the head of the pier or mole leading to the island of Pharos, which was without Caesar's lines, and still in the hands of the Egyptian authorities. The Egyptians thus commanded the entrance to the mole. The island itself, also, with the fortress at the other end of the pier, was still in the possession of the Egyptian authorities, who seemed disposed to hold it for Achillas. The mole was very long, as the island was nearly a mile from the shore. There was quite a little town upon the island itself, besides the fortress or castle built there to defend the place. The garrison of this castle was strong, and the inhabitants of the town, too, constituted a somewhat formidable population, as they consisted of fishermen, sailors, wreckers, and such other desperate characters, as usually congregate about such a spot. Cleopatra and Caesar, from the windows of their palace within the city, looked out upon this island, with the tall light house rising in the center of it and the castle at its base, and upon the long and narrow isthmus connecting it with the main land, and concluded that it was very essential that they should get possession of the post, commanding, as it did, the entrance to the harbor.

In the harbor, which was on the south side of the mole, and, consequently, on the side opposite to that from which Achillas was advancing toward the city, there were lying a large number of Egyptian vessels, some dismantled, and others manned and armed more or less effectively. These vessels had not yet come into Achillas's hands, but it would be certain that he would take possession of them as soon as he should gain admittance to those parts of the city which Caesar had abandoned. This it was extremely important to prevent; for, if Achillas held this fleet, especially if he continued to command the island of Pharos, he would be perfect master of all the approaches to the city on the side of the sea. He could then not only receive re-enforcements and supplies himself from that quarter, but he could also effectually cut off the Roman army from all possibility of receiving any. It became, therefore, as

Caesar thought, imperiously necessary that he should protect himself from this danger. This he did by sending out an expedition to burn all the shipping in the harbor, and, at the same time, to take possession of a certain fort upon the island of Pharos which commanded the entrance to the port. This undertaking was abundantly successful. The troops burned the shipping, took the fort, expelled the Egyptian soldiers from it, and put a Roman garrison into it instead, and then returned in safety within Caesar's lines. Cleopatra witnessed these exploits from her palace windows with feelings of the highest admiration for the energy and valor which her Roman protectors displayed.

The burning of the Egyptian ships in this action, however fortunate for Cleopatra and Caesar, was attended with a catastrophe which has ever since been lamented by the whole civilized world. Some of the burning ships were driven by the wind to the shore, where they set fire to the buildings which were contiguous to the water. The flames spread and produced an extensive conflagration, in the course of which the largest part of the great library was destroyed. This library was the only general collection of the ancient writings that ever had been made, and the loss of it was never repaired.

The destruction of the Egyptian fleet resulted also in the downfall and ruin of Achillas. From the time of Arsinoe's arrival in the camp there had been a constant rivalry and jealousy between himself and Ganymede, the eunuch who had accompanied Arsinoe in her flight. Two parties had been formed in the army, some declaring for Achillas and some for Ganymede. Arsinoe advocated Ganymede's interests, and when, at length, the fleet was burned, she charged Achillas with having been, by his neglect or incapacity, the cause of the loss. Achillas was tried, condemned, and beheaded. From that time Ganymede assumed the administration of Arsinoe's government as her minister of state and the commander-in-chief of her armies.

About the time that these occurrences took place, the Egyptian army advanced into those parts of the city from which Caesar had withdrawn, producing those terrible scenes of panic and confusion which always attend a sudden and violent change of military possession within the precincts of a city. Ganymede brought up his troops on every side to the walls of Caesar's citadels and intrenchments, and hemmed him closely in. He cut off all avenues of approach to Caesar's lines by land, and commenced vigorous preparations for an assault. He constructed engines for battering down the walls. He opened shops and established forges in every part of the city for the manufacture of darts, spears, pikes, and all kinds of military machinery. He built towers supported upon huge wheels, with the design of filling them with armed men when finally ready to make his assault upon Caesar's lines, and moving them up to the walls of the citadels and palaces, so as to give to his soldiers the advantage of a lofty elevation in making their attacks. He levied contributions on the rich citizens for the necessary funds, and provided himself with men by pressing all the artisans, laborers, and men capable of bearing arms into his service. He sent messengers back into the interior of the country, in every direction, summoning the people to arms, and calling for contributions of money and military stores.

These messengers were instructed to urge upon the people that, unless Caesar and his army were at once expelled from Alexandria, there was imminent danger that the national independence of Egypt would be forever destroyed. The Romans, they were to say, had extended their conquests over almost all the rest of the world. They had sent one army into Egypt before, under the command of Mark Antony, under the pretense of restoring Ptolemy Auletes to the throne. Now another commander, with another force, had come, offering some other pretexts for interfering in their affairs. These Roman encroachments, the messengers were to say, would end in the complete subjugation of Egypt to a foreign power, unless the people of the country aroused themselves to meet the danger manfully, and to expel the intruders.

As Caesar had possession of the island of Pharos and of the harbor, Ganymede could not cut him off from receiving such re-enforcements of men and arms as he might make arrangements for obtaining beyond the sea; nor could he curtail his supply of food, as the granaries and magazines within Caesar's quarter of the city contained almost inexhaustible stores of corn. There was one remaining point essential to the subsistence of an army besieged, and that was an abundant supply of water. The palaces and citadels which Caesar occupied were supplied with water by means of numerous subterranean aqueducts, which conveyed the water from the Nile to vast cisterns built under ground, whence it was raised by buckets and hydraulic engines for use. In reflecting upon this circumstance, Ganymede conceived the design of secretly digging a canal, so as to turn the waters of the sea by means of it into these aqueducts. This plan he carried into effect. The consequence was, that the water in the cisterns was gradually changed. It became first brackish, then more and more salt and bitter, until, at length, it was wholly impossible to use it. For some time the army within could not understand these changes; and when, at length, they discovered the cause the soldiers were panic-stricken at the thought that they were now apparently wholly at the mercy of their enemies, since, without supplies of water, they must all immediately perish. They considered it hopeless to attempt any longer to hold out, and urged Caesar to evacuate the city, embark on board his galleys, and proceed to sea.

Instead of doing this, however, Caesar, ordering all other operations to be suspended, employed the whole laboring force of his command, under the direction of the captains of the several companies, in digging wells in every part of his quarter of the city. Fresh water, he said, was almost invariably found, at a moderate depth, upon sea-coasts, even upon ground lying in very close proximity to the sea. The digging was successful. Fresh water, in great abundance, was found. Thus this danger was passed, and the men's fears effectually relieved.

A short time after these transactions occurred, there came into the harbor one day, from along the shore west of the city, a small sloop, bringing the intelligence that a squadron of transports had arrived upon the coast to the westward of Alexandria, and had anchored there, being unable to come up to the city on account of an easterly wind which prevailed at that season of the year. This squadron was one which had been sent across the Mediterranean with arms, ammunition, and military stores for Caesar, in answer to requisitions which he had made immediately after he had landed. The transports being thus windbound on the coast, and having nearly exhausted their supplies of water, were in distress; and they accordingly sent forward the sloop, which was probably propelled by oars, to make known their situation to Caesar, and to ask for succor. Caesar immediately went, himself, on board of one of his galleys, and ordering the remainder of his little fleet to follow him, he set sail out of the harbor, and then turned to the westward, with a view of proceeding along the coast to the place where the transports were lying.

All this was done secretly. The land is so low in the vicinity of Alexandria that boats or galleys are out of sight from it at a very short distance from the shore. In fact, travelers say that, in coming upon the coast, the illusion produced by the spherical form of the surface of the water and the low and level character of the coast is such that one seems actually to descend from the sea to the land. Caesar might therefore have easily kept his expedition a secret, had it not been that, in order to be provided with a supply of water for the transports immediately on reaching them, he stopped at a solitary part of the coast, at some distance from Alexandria, and sent a party a little way into the interior in search for water. This party were discovered by the country people, and were intercepted by a troop of horse and made prisoners. From these prisoners the Egyptians learned that Caesar himself was on the coast with a small squadron of galleys. The tidings spread in all directions. The people flocked together from every quarter. They hastily collected all the boats and vessels which could be obtained at the villages in that region and from the various branches of the Nile. In the mean time, Caesar had gone on to the anchorage ground of the squadron, and had taken the transports in tow to bring them to the city; for the galleys, being propelled by oars, were in a measure independent of the wind. On his return, he found quite a formidable naval armament assembled to dispute the passage.

A severe conflict ensued, but Caesar was victorious. The navy which the Egyptians had so suddenly got together was as suddenly destroyed. Some of the vessels were burned, others sunk, and others captured; and Caesar returned in triumph to the port with his transports and stores. He was welcomed with the acclamations of his soldiers, and, still more warmly, by the joy and gratitude of Cleopatra, who had been waiting during his absence in great anxiety and suspense to know the result of the expedition, aware as she was that her hero was exposing himself in it to the most imminent personal danger.

The arrival of these re-enforcements greatly improved Caesar's condition, and the circumstance of their coming forced upon the mind of Ganymede a sense of the absolute necessity that he should gain possession of the harbor if he intended to keep Caesar in check. He accordingly determined to take immediate measures for forming a naval force. He sent along the coast, and ordered every ship and galley that could be found in all the ports to be sent immediately to Alexandria. He employed as many men as possible in and around the city in building more. He unroofed some of the most magnificent edifices to procure timber as a material for making benches and oars. When all was ready, he made a grand attack upon Caesar in the port, and a terrible contest ensued for the possession of the harbor, the mole, the island, and the citadels and fortresses commanding the entrances from the sea. Caesar well knew this contest would be a decisive one in respect to the final result of the war, and he accordingly went forth himself to take an active and personal part in the conflict. He felt doubtless, too, a strong emotion of pride and pleasure in exhibiting his prowess in the sight of Cleopatra, who could watch the progress of the battle from the palace windows, full of excitement at the dangers which he incurred, and of admiration at the feats of strength and valor which he performed. During this battle the life of the great conqueror was several times in the most imminent danger. He wore a habit or mantle of the imperial purple, which made him a conspicuous mark for his enemies; and, of course, wherever he went, in that place was the hottest of the fight. Once, in the midst of a scene of most dreadful confusion and din, he leaped from an overloaded boat into the water and swam for his life, holding his cloak between his teeth and drawing it through the water after him, that it might not fall into the hands of his enemies. He carried, at the same time, as he swam, certain valuable papers which he wished to save, holding them above his head with one hand, while he propelled himself through the water with the other.

The result of this contest was another decisive victory for Caesar. Not only were the ships which the Egyptians had collected defeated and destroyed, but the mole, with the fortresses at each extremity of it, and the island, with the light house and the town of Pharos, all fell into Caesar's hands.

The Egyptians now began to be discouraged. The army and the people, judging, as mankind always do, of the virtue of their military commanders solely by the criterion of success, began to be tired of the rule of Ganymede and Arsinoe. They sent secret messengers to Caesar avowing their discontent, and saying that, if he would liberate Ptolemy—who, it will be recollected, had been all this time held as a sort of prisoner of state in Caesar's palaces—they thought that the people generally would receive him as their sovereign, and that then an arrangement might easily be made for an amicable adjustment of the whole controversy. Caesar was strongly inclined to accede to this proposal.

He accordingly called Ptolemy into his presence and, taking him kindly by the hand, informed him of the wishes of the people of Egypt, and gave him permission to go. Ptolemy, however, begged not to be sent away. He professed the strongest attachment to Caesar, and the utmost confidence in him, and he very much preferred, he said, to remain under his protection. Caesar replied that, if those were his sentiments, the separation would not be a lasting one. "If we part as friends," he said, "we shall soon meet again." By these and similar assurances he endeavored to encourage the young prince, and then sent him away. Ptolemy was received by the Egyptians with great joy, and was immediately placed at the head of the government. Instead, however, of endeavoring to promote a settlement of the quarrel with Caesar, he seemed to enter into it now himself, personally, with the utmost ardor, and began at once to make the most extensive preparations both by sea and land for a vigorous prosecution of the war. What the result of these operations would have been can now not be known, for the general aspect of affairs was, soon after these transactions, totally changed by the occurrence of a new and very important event which suddenly intervened, and which turned the attention of all parties, both Egyptians and Romans, to the eastern quarter of the kingdom. The tidings arrived that a large army under the command of a general named Mithradates, whom Caesar had dispatched into Asia for this purpose, had suddenly appeared at Pelusium, had captured that city and were now ready to march to Alexandria.

The Egyptian army immediately broke up its encampments in the neighborhood of Alexandria, and marched to the eastward to meet these new invaders. Caesar followed them with all the forces that he could safely take away from the city. He left the city in the night, and unobserved, and moved across the country with such celerity that he joined Mithradates before the forces of Ptolemy had arrived. After various marches and maneuvers, the armies met, and a great battle was fought. The Egyptians were defeated. Ptolemy's camp was taken. As the Roman army burst in upon one side of it, the guards and attendants of Ptolemy fled upon the other, clambering over the ramparts in the utmost terror and confusion. The foremost fell headlong into the ditch below, which was thus soon filled to the brim with the dead and the dying; while those who came behind pressed on over the bridge thus formed, trampling remorselessly, as they fled, on the bodies of their comrades, who lay writhing, struggling, and shrieking beneath their feet. Those who escaped reached the river. They crowded together into a boat which lay at the bank and pushed off from the shore. The boat was overloaded, and it sank as soon as it left the land. The Romans drew the bodies which floated to the shore upon the bank again, and they found among them one, which, by the royal cuirass which was upon it, the customary badge and armor of the Egyptian kings, they knew to be the body of Ptolemy.

The victory which Caesar obtained in this battle and the death of Ptolemy ended the war. Nothing now remained but for him to place himself at the head of the combined forces and march back to Alexandria. The Egyptian forces which had been left there made no resistance, and he entered the city in triumph. He took Arsinoe prisoner. He decreed that Cleopatra should reign as queen, and that she should marry her youngest brother, the other Ptolemy,—a boy at this time about eleven years of age. A marriage with one so young was, of course, a mere form. Cleopatra remained, as before, the companion of Caesar.

Caesar had, in the mean time, incurred great censure at Rome, and throughout the whole Roman world, for having thus turned aside from his own proper duties as the Roman consul, and the commander-in-chief of the armies of the empire, to embroil himself in the quarrels of a remote and secluded kingdom with which the interests of the Roman commonwealth were so little connected. His friends and the authorities at Rome were continually urging him to return. They were especially indignant at his protracted neglect of his own proper duties, from knowing that he was held in Egypt by a guilty attachment to the queen,—thus not only violating his obligations to the state, but likewise inflicting upon his wife Calpurnia, and his family at Rome, an intolerable wrong. But Caesar was so fascinated by Cleopatra's charms, and by the mysterious and unaccountable influence which she exercised over him, that he paid no heed to any of these remonstrances. Even after the war was ended he remained some months in Egypt to enjoy his favorite's society. He would spend whole nights in her company, in feasting and revelry. He made a splendid royal progress with her through Egypt after the war was over, attended by a numerous train of Roman guards. He formed a plan for taking her to Rome, and marrying her there; and he took measures for having the laws of the city altered so as to enable him to do so, though he was already married.

All these things produced great discontent and disaffection among Caesar's friends and throughout the Roman army. The Egyptians, too, strongly censured the conduct of Cleopatra. A son was born to her about this time, whom the Alexandrians named, from his father, Caesarion. Cleopatra was regarded in the new relation of mother, which she now sustained, not with interest and sympathy, but with feelings of reproach and condemnation.

Cleopatra was all this time growing more and more accomplished, and more and more beautiful; but her vivacity and spirit, which had been so charming while it was simple and childlike, now began to appear more forward and bold. It is the characteristic of pure and lawful love to soften and subdue the heart, and infuse a gentle and quiet spirit into all its action; while that which breaks over the barriers that God and nature have marked out for it, tends to make woman masculine and bold, to indurate all her sensibilities, and to destroy that gentleness and timidity of demeanor which have so great an influence in heightening her charms. Cleopatra was beginning to experience these effects. She was indifferent to the opinions of her subjects, and was only anxious to maintain as long as possible her guilty ascendency over Caesar.

Caesar, however, finally determined to set out on his return to the capital. Leaving Cleopatra, accordingly, a sufficient force to secure the continuance of her power, he embarked the remainder of his forces in his transports and galleys, and sailed away. He took the unhappy Arsinoe with him, intending to exhibit her as a trophy of his Egyptian victories on his arrival at Rome.

CHAPTER VIII.

CLEOPATRA A QUEEN.

The Alexandrine war very short.—Its extent.—Revenues of Egypt.—The city repaired.—The library rebuilt.—A new collection of manuscripts.— Luxury and splendor.—Deterioration of Cleopatra's character.—The young Ptolemy. —Cleopatra assassinates him.—Career of Caesar.—His rapid course of conquest.—Cleopatra determines to go to Rome.—Feelings of the Romans.— Caesar's four triumphs.—Nature of triumphal processions.—Arsinoe.— Sympathy of the Roman people.—Caesar overacts his part.—Feasts and festivals.—Riot and debauchery.—Public combats.—The artificial lake.— Combat upon it.—Land combats.—The people shocked.—Cleopatra's visit. —Caesar's plans for making himself king.—Conspiracy against Caesar.—He is assassinated.—Arsinoe released.—Calpurnia mourns her husband's death. —Calpurnia looks to Mark Antony as her protector.

The war by which Caesar reinstated Cleopatra upon the throne was not one of very long duration. Caesar arrived in Egypt in pursuit of Pompey about the first of August; the war was ended and Cleopatra established in secure possession by the end of January; so that the conflict, violent as it was while it continued, was very brief, the peaceful and commercial pursuits of the Alexandrians having been interrupted by it only for a few months.

Nor did either the war itself, or the derangements consequent upon it, extend very far into the interior of the country. The city of Alexandria itself and the neighboring coasts were the chief scenes of the contest until Mithradates arrived at Pelusium. He, it is true, marched across the Delta, and the final battle was fought in the interior of the country. It was, however, after all, but a very small portion of the Egyptian territory that was directly affected by the war. The great mass of the people, occupying the rich and fertile tracts which bordered the various branches of the Nile, and the long and verdant valley which extended so far into the heart of the continent, knew nothing of the conflict but by vague and distant rumors. The pursuits of the agricultural population went on, all the time, as steadily and prosperously as ever; so that when the conflict was ended, and Cleopatra entered upon the quiet and peaceful possession of her power, she found that the resources of her empire were very little impaired.

She availed herself, accordingly, of the revenues which poured in very abundantly upon her, to enter upon a career of the greatest luxury, magnificence, and splendor. The injuries which had been done to the palaces and other public edifices of Alexandria by the fire, and by the military operations of the siege, were repaired. The bridges which had been broken down were rebuilt. The canals which had been obstructed were opened again. The sea-water was shut off from the palace cisterns; the rubbish of demolished houses was removed; the barricades were cleared from the streets; and the injuries which the palaces had suffered either from the violence of military engines or the rough occupation of the Roman soldiery, were repaired. In a word, the city was speedily restored once more, so far as was possible, to its former order and beauty. The five hundred thousand manuscripts of the Alexandrian library, which had been burned, could not, indeed, be restored; but, in all other respects, the city soon resumed in appearance all its former splendor. Even in respect to the library, Cleopatra made an effort to retrieve the loss. She repaired the ruined buildings, and afterward, in the course of her life, she brought together, it was said, in a manner hereafter to be described, one or two hundred thousand rolls of manuscripts, as the commencement of a new collection. The new library, however, never acquired the fame and distinction that had pertained to the old.

The former sovereigns of Egypt, Cleopatra's ancestors, had generally, as has already been shown, devoted the immense revenues which they extorted from the agriculturalists of the valley of the Nile to purposes of ambition. Cleopatra seemed now disposed to expend them in luxury and pleasure. They, the Ptolemies, had employed their resources in erecting vast structures, or founding magnificent institutions at Alexandria, to add to the glory of the city, and to widen and extend their own fame. Cleopatra, on the other hand, as was, perhaps, naturally to be expected of a young, beautiful, and impulsive woman suddenly raised to so conspicuous a position, and to the possession of such unbounded wealth and power, expended her royal revenues in plans of personal display, and in scenes of festivity, gayety, and enjoyment. She adorned her palaces, built magnificent barges for pleasure excursions on the Nile, and expended enormous sums for dress, for equipages, and for sumptuous entertainments. In fact, so lavish were her expenditures for these and similar purposes during the early years of her reign, that she is considered as having carried the extravagance of sensual luxury, and personal display, and splendor, beyond the limits that had ever before or have ever since been attained.

Whatever of simplicity of character, and of gentleness and kindness of spirit she might have possessed in her earlier years, of course gradually disappeared under the influences of such a course of life as she now was leading. She was beautiful and fascinating still, but she began to grow selfish, heartless, and designing. Her little brother,—he was but eleven years of age, it will be recollected, when Caesar arranged the marriage between them,—was an object of jealousy to her. He was now, of course, too young to take any actual share in the exercise of the royal power, or to interfere at all in his sister's plans or pleasures. But then he was growing older. In a few years he would be fifteen,—which was the period of life fixed upon by Caesar's arrangements, and, in fact, by the laws and usages of the Egyptian kingdom,—when he was to come into possession of power as king, and as the husband of Cleopatra. Cleopatra was extremely unwilling that the change in her relations to him and to the government, which this period was to bring, should take place. Accordingly, just before the time arrived, she caused him to be poisoned. His death released her, as she had intended, from all restraints, and thereafter she continued to reign alone. During the remainder of her life, so far as the enjoyment of wealth and power, and of all other elements of external prosperity could go, Cleopatra's career was one of uninterrupted success. She had no conscientious scruples to interfere with the most full and unrestrained indulgence of every propensity of her heart, and the means of indulgence were before her in the most unlimited profusion. The only bar to her happiness was the impossibility of satisfying the impulses and passions of the human soul, when they once break over the bounds which the laws both of God and of nature ordain for restraining them.

In the mean time, while Cleopatra was spending the early years of her reign in all this luxury and splendor, Caesar was pursuing his career, as the conqueror of the world, in the most successful manner. On the death of Pompey, he would naturally have succeeded at once to the enjoyment of the supreme power; but his delay in Egypt, and the extent to which it was known that he was entangled with Cleopatra, encouraged and strengthened his enemies in various parts of the world. In fact, a revolt which broke out in Asia Minor, and which it was absolutely necessary that he should proceed at once to quell, was the immediate cause of his leaving Egypt at last. Other plans for making head against Caesar's power were formed in Spain, in Africa, and in Italy. His military skill and energy, however, were so great, and the ascendency which he exercised over the minds of men by his personal presence was so unbounded, and so astonishing, moreover, was the celerity with which he moved from continent to continent, and from kingdom to kingdom, that in a very short period from the time of his leaving Egypt, he had conducted most brilliant and successful campaigns in all the three quarters of the world then known, had put down effectually all opposition to his power, and then had returned to Rome the acknowledged master of the world. Cleopatra, who had, of course, watched his career during all this time with great pride and pleasure, concluded, at last, to go to Rome and make a visit to him there.

The people of Rome were, however, not prepared to receive her very cordially. It was an age in which vice of every kind was regarded with great indulgence, but the moral instincts of mankind were too strong to be wholly blinded to the true character of so conspicuous an example of wickedness as this. Arsinoe was at Rome, too, during this period of Caesar's life. He had brought her there, it will be recollected, on his return from Egypt, as a prisoner, and as a trophy of his victory. His design was, in fact, to reserve her as a captive to grace his *triumph*.

A triumph, according to the usages of the ancient Romans, was a grand celebration decreed by the Senate to great military commanders of the highest rank, when they returned from distant campaigns in which they had made great conquests or gained extraordinary victories. Caesar concentrated all his triumphs into one. They were celebrated on his return to Rome for the last time, after having completed the conquest of the world. The processions of this triumph occupied four days. In fact, there were four triumphs, one on each day for the four days. The wars and conquests which these ovations were intended to celebrate were those of Gaul, of Egypt, of Asia, and of Africa; and the processions on the several days consisted of endless trains of prisoners, trophies, arms, banners, pictures, images, convoys of wagons loaded with plunder, captive princes and princesses, animals wild and tame, and every thing else which the conqueror had been able to bring home with him from his campaigns, to excite the curiosity or the admiration of the people of the city and illustrate the magnitude of his exploits. Of course, the Roman generals, when engaged in distant foreign wars, were ambitious of bringing back as many distinguished captives and as much public plunder as they were able to obtain, in order to add to the variety and splendor of the triumphal procession by which their victories were to be honored on their return. It was with this view that Caesar brought Arsinoe from Egypt; and he had retained her as his captive at Rome until his conquests were completed and the time for his triumph arrived. She, of course, formed a part of the triumphal train on the *Egyptian* day. She walked immediately before the chariot in which Caesar rode. She was in chains, like any other captive, though her chains in honor of her lofty rank, were made of gold.

The effect, however, upon the Roman population of seeing the unhappy princess, overwhelmed as she was with sorrow and chagrin, as she moved slowly along in the train, among the other emblems and trophies of violence and plunder, proved to be by no means favorable to Caesar. The population were inclined to pity her, and to sympathize with her in her sufferings. The sight of her distress recalled too, to their minds, the dereliction from duty which Caesar had been guilty of in his yielding to the enticements of Cleopatra, and remaining so long in Egypt to the neglect of his proper duties as a Roman minister of state. In a word, the tide of admiration for Caesar's military exploits which had been setting so strongly in his favor, seemed inclined to turn, and the city was filled with murmurs against him even in the midst of his triumphs.

In fact, the pride and vainglory which led Caesar to make his triumphs more splendid and imposing than any former conqueror had ever enjoyed, caused him to overact his part so as to produce effects the reverse of his intentions. The case of Arsinoe was one example of this. Instead of impressing the people with a sense of the greatness of his exploits in Egypt, in deposing one queen and bringing her captive to Rome, in order that he might place another upon the throne in her stead, it only reproduced anew the censures and criminations which he had deserved by his actions there, but which, had it not been for the pitiable spectacle of Arsinoe in the train, might have been forgotten.

There were other examples of a similar character. There were the feasts, for instance. From the plunder which Caesar had obtained in his various campaigns, he expended the most enormous sums in making feasts and spectacles for the populace at the time of his triumph. A large portion of the populace was pleased, it is true, with the boundless indulgences thus offered to them; but the better part of the Roman people were indignant at the waste and extravagance which were every where displayed. For many days the whole city of Rome presented to the view nothing but one wide-spread scene of riot and debauchery. The people, instead of being pleased with this abundance, said that Caesar must have practiced the most extreme and lawless extortion to have obtained the vast amount of money necessary to enable him to supply such unbounded and reckless waste.

There was another way, too, by which Caesar turned public opinion strongly against himself, by the very means which he adopted for creating a sentiment in his favor. The Romans, among the other barbarous amusements which were practiced in the city, were specially fond of combats. These combats were of various kinds. They were fought sometimes between ferocious beasts of the same or of different species, as dogs against each other, or against bulls, lions, or tigers. Any animals, in fact, were employed for this purpose, that could be teased or goaded into anger and ferocity in a fight. Sometimes men were employed in these combats,—captive soldiers, that had been taken in war, and brought to Rome to fight in the amphitheaters there as gladiators. These men were compelled to contend sometimes with wild beasts, and sometimes with one another. Caesar, knowing how highly the Roman assemblies enjoyed such scenes, determined to afford them the indulgence on a most magnificent scale, supposing, of course, that the greater and the more dreadful the fight, the higher would be the pleasure which the spectators would enjoy in witnessing it. Accordingly, in making preparations for the festivities attending his triumph, he caused a large artificial lake to be formed at a convenient place in the vicinity of Rome, where it could be surrounded by the populace of the city, and there he made arrangements for a naval battle. A great number of galleys were introduced into the lake. They were of the usual size employed in war. These galleys were manned with numerous soldiers. Tyrian captives were put upon one side, and Egyptian upon the other; and when all was ready, the two squadrons were ordered to approach and fight a real battle for the amusement of the enormous throngs of spectators that were assembled around. As the nations from which the combatants in this conflict were respectively taken were hostile to each other, and as the men fought, of course, for their lives, the engagement was attended with the usual horrors of a desperate naval encounter. Hundreds were slain. The dead bodies of the combatants fell from the galleys into the lake and the waters of it were dyed with their blood.

There were land combats, too, on the same grand scale. In one of them five hundred foot soldiers, twenty elephants, and a troop of thirty horse were engaged on each side. This combat, therefore, was an action greater, in respect to the number of the combatants, than the famous battle of Lexington, which marked the commencement of the American war; and in respect to the slaughter which took place, it was very probably ten times greater. The horror of these scenes proved to be too much even for the populace, fierce and merciless as it was, which they were intended to amuse. Caesar, in his eagerness to outdo all former exhibitions and shows, went beyond the limits within which the seeing of men butchered in bloody combats and dying in agony and despair would serve for a pleasure and a pastime. The people were shocked; and condemnations of Caesar's cruelty were added to the other suppressed reproaches and criminations which every where arose.

Cleopatra, during her visit to Rome, lived openly with Caesar at his residence, and this excited very general displeasure. In fact, while the people pitied Arsinoe, Cleopatra, notwithstanding her beauty and her thousand personal accomplishments and charms, was an object of general displeasure, so far as public attention was turned toward her at all. The public mind was, however, much engrossed by the great political movements made by Caesar and the ends toward which he seemed to be aiming. Men accused him of designing to be made a king. Parties were formed for and against him; and though men did not dare openly to utter their sentiments, their passions became the more violent in proportion to the external force by which they were suppressed. Mark Antony was at Rome at this time. He warmly espoused Caesar's cause, and encouraged his design of making himself king. He once, in fact, offered to place a royal diadem upon Caesar's head at some public celebration; but the marks of public disapprobation which the act elicited caused him to desist.

At length, however, the time arrived when Caesar determined to cause himself to be proclaimed king. He took advantage of a certain remarkable conjuncture of public affairs, which can not here be particularly described, but which seemed to him specially to favor his designs, and arrangements were made for having him invested with the regal power by the Senate. The murmurs and the discontent of the people at the indications that the time for the realization of their fears was drawing nigh, became more and more audible, and at length a conspiracy was formed to put an end to the danger by destroying the ambitious aspirant's life. Two stern and determined men, Brutus and Cassius, were the leaders of this conspiracy. They matured their plans, organized their band of associates, provided themselves secretly with arms, and when the Senate convened, on the day in which the decisive vote was to have been passed, Caesar himself presiding, they came up boldly around him in his presidential chair, and murdered him with their daggers.

Antony, from whom the plans of the conspirators had been kept profoundly secret, stood by, looking on stupefied and confounded while the deed was done, but utterly unable to render his friend any protection.

Cleopatra immediately fled from the city and returned to Egypt.

Arsinoe had gone away before. Caesar, either taking pity on her misfortunes, or impelled, perhaps, by the force of public sentiment, which seemed inclined to take part with her against him, set her at liberty immediately after the ceremonies of his triumph were over. He would not, however, allow her to return into Egypt, for fear, probably, that she might in some way or other be the means of disturbing the government of Cleopatra. She proceeded, accordingly, into Syria, no longer as a captive, but still as an exile from her native land. We shall hereafter learn what became of her there.

Calpurnia mourned the death of her husband with sincere and unaffected grief. She bore the wrongs which she suffered as a wife with a very patient and unrepining spirit, and loved her husband with the most devoted attachment to the end. Nothing can be more affecting than the proofs of her tender and anxious regard on the night immediately preceding the assassination. There were certain slight and obscure indications of danger which her watchful devotion to her husband led her to observe, though they eluded the notice of all Caesar's other friends, and they filled her with apprehension and anxiety; and when at length the bloody body was brought home to her from the senate-house, she was overwhelmed with grief and despair.

She had no children. She accordingly looked upon Mark Antony as her nearest friend and protector, and in the confusion and terror which prevailed the next day in the city, she hastily packed together the money and other valuables contained in the house, and all her husband's books and papers, and sent them to Antony for safe keeping.

CHAPTER IX.

THE BATTLE OF PHILIPPI.

Consternation at Rome.—Caesar's will.—Brutus and Cassius.—Parties formed.—Octavius and Lepidus.—Character of Octavius.—Octavius proceeds to Rome.—He claims his rights as heir.—Lepidus takes command of the army.—The triumvirate.—Conference between Octavius, Lepidus, and

When the tidings of the assassination of Caesar were first announced to the people of Rome, all ranks and classes of men were struck with amazement and consternation. No one knew what to say or do. A very large and influential portion of the community had been Caesar's friends. It was equally certain that there was a very powerful interest opposed to him. No one could foresee which of these two parties would now carry the day, and, of course, for a time, all was uncertainty and indecision.

Mark Antony came forward at once, and assumed the position of Caesar's representative and the leader of the party on that side. A will was found among Caesar's effects, and when the will was opened it appeared that large sums of money were left to the Roman people, and other large amounts to a nephew of the deceased, named Octavius, who will be more particularly spoken of hereafter. Antony was named in the will as the executor of it. This and other circumstances seemed to authorize him to come forward as the head and the leader of the Caesar party. Brutus and Cassius, who remained openly in the city after their desperate deed had been performed, were the acknowledged leaders of the other party; while the mass of the people were at first so astounded at the magnitude and suddenness of the revolution which the open and public assassination of a Roman emperor by a Roman Senate denoted, that they knew not what to say or do. In fact, the killing of Julius Caesar, considering the exalted position which he occupied, the rank and station of the men who perpetrated the deed, and the very extraordinary publicity of the scene in which the act was performed, was, doubtless, the most conspicuous and most appalling case of assassination that has ever occurred. The whole population of Rome seemed for some days to be amazed and stupefied by the tidings. At length, however, parties began to be more distinctly formed. The lines of demarkation between them were gradually drawn, and men began to arrange themselves more and more unequivocally on the opposite sides.

For a short time the supremacy of Antony over the Caesar party was readily acquiesced in and allowed. At length, however, and before his arrangements were finally matured, he found that he had two formidable competitors upon his own side. These were Octavius and Lepidus.

Octavius, who was the nephew of Caesar, already alluded to, was a very accomplished and elegant young man, now about nineteen years of age. He was the son of Julius Caesar's niece.[1]

> [Footnote 1: This Octavius on his subsequent elevation to imperial power, received the name of Augustus Caesar, and it is by this name that he is generally known in history. He was, however, called Octavius at the commencement of his career, and, to avoid confusion, we shall continue to designate him by this name to the end of our narrative.]

He had always been a great favorite with his uncle. Every possible attention had been paid to his education, and he had been advanced by Caesar, already, to positions of high importance in public life. Caesar, in fact, adopted him as his son, and made him his heir. At the time of Caesar's death he was at Apollonia, a city of Illyricum, north of Greece. The troops under his command there offered to march at once with him, if he wished it, to Rome, and avenge his uncle's death. Octavius, after some hesitation, concluded that it would be most prudent for him to proceed thither first himself, alone, as a private person, and demand his rights as his uncle's heir, according to the provisions of the will. He accordingly did so. He found, on his arrival, that the will, the property, the books and parchments, and the substantial power of the government, were all in Antony's hands. Antony, instead of putting Octavius into possession of his property and rights, found various pretexts for evasion and delay. Octavius was too young yet, he said, to assume such weighty responsibilities. He was himself also too much pressed with the urgency of public affairs to attend to the business of the will. With these and similar excuses as his justification, Antony seemed inclined to pay no regard whatever to Octavius's claims.

Octavius, young as he was, possessed a character that was marked with great intelligence, spirit, and resolution. He soon made many powerful friends in the city of Rome and among the Roman Senate. It became a serious question whether he or Antony would gain the greatest ascendency in the party of Caesar's friends. The contest for this ascendency was, in fact, protracted for two or three years, and led to a vast complication of intrigues, and maneuvers, and civil wars, which can not, however, be here particularly detailed.

The other competitor which Antony had to contend with was a distinguished Roman general named Lepidus. Lepidus was an officer of the army, in very high command at the time of Caesar's death. He was present in the senate-chamber on the day of the assassination. He stole secretly away when he saw that the deed was done, and repaired to the camp of the army without the city and immediately assumed the command of the forces. This gave him great power, and in the course of the contests which subsequently ensued between Antony and Octavius, he took an active part, and held in some measure the balance between them. At length the contest was finally closed by a coalition of the three rivals. Finding that they could not either of them gain a decided victory over the others, they combined together, and formed the celebrated *triumvirate*, which continued afterward for some time to wield the supreme command in the Roman world. In forming this league of reconciliation, the three rivals held their conference on an island situated in one of the branches of the Po, in the north of Italy. They manifested extreme jealousy and suspicion of each other in coming to this interview. Two bridges were built leading to the island, one from each bank of the stream. The army of Antony was drawn up upon one side of the river, and that of Octavius upon the other. Lepidus went first to the island by one of the bridges. After examining the ground carefully, to make himself sure that it contained no ambuscade, he made a signal to the other generals, who then came over, each advancing by his own bridge, and accompanied by three hundred guards, who remained upon the bridge to secure a retreat for their masters in case of treachery. The conference lasted three days, at the expiration of which time the articles were all agreed upon and signed.

This league being formed, the three confederates turned their united force against the party of the conspirators. Of this party Brutus and Cassius were still at the head.

The scene of the contests between Octavius, Antony, and Lepidus had been chiefly Italy and the other central countries of Europe. Brutus and Cassius, on the other hand, had gone across the Adriatic Sea into the East immediately after Caesar's assassination. They were now in Asia Minor, and were employed in concentrating their forces, forming alliances with the various Eastern powers, raising troops, bringing over to their side the Roman legions which were stationed in that quarter of the world, seizing magazines, and exacting contributions from all who could be induced to favor their cause. Among other embassages which they sent, one went to Egypt to demand aid from Cleopatra. Cleopatra, however, was resolved to join the other side in the contest. It was natural that she should feel grateful to Caesar for his efforts and sacrifices in her behalf, and that she should be inclined to favor the cause of his friends. Accordingly, instead of sending troops to aid Brutus and Cassius, as they had desired her to do, she immediately fitted out an expedition to proceed to the coast of Asia, with a view of rendering all the aid in her power to Antony's cause.

Cassius, on his part, finding that Cleopatra was determined on joining his enemies, immediately resolved on proceeding at once to Egypt and taking possession of the country. He also stationed a military force at Taenarus, the southern promontory of Greece, to watch for and intercept the fleet of Cleopatra as soon as it should appear on the European shores. All these plans, however—both those which Cleopatra formed against Cassius, and those which Cassius formed against her—failed of accomplishment. Cleopatra's fleet encountered a terrible storm, which dispersed and destroyed it. A small remnant was driven upon the coast of Africa, but nothing could be saved which could be made available for the purpose intended. As for Cassius's intended expedition to Egypt, it was not carried into effect. The dangers which began now to threaten him from the direction of Italy and Rome were so imminent, that, at Brutus's urgent request, he gave up the Egyptian plan, and the two generals concentrated their forces to meet the armies of the triumvirate which were now rapidly advancing to attack them. They passed for this purpose across the Hellespont from Sestos to Abydos, and entered Thrace.

After various marches and countermarches, and a long succession of those maneuvers by which two powerful armies, approaching a contest, endeavor each to gain some position of advantage against the other, the various bodies of troops belonging, respectively, to the two powers, came into the vicinity of each other near Philippi. Brutus and Cassius arrived here first. There was a plain in the neighborhood of the city, with a rising ground in a certain portion of it. Brutus took possession of this elevation, and intrenched himself there. Cassius posted his forces about three miles distant, near the sea. There was a line of intrenchments between the two camps, which formed a chain of communication by which the positions of the two commanders were connected. The armies were thus very advantageously posted. They had the River Strymon and a marsh on the left of the ground that they occupied, while the plain was before them, and the sea behind. Here they awaited the arrival of their foes.

Antony, who was at this time at Amphipolis, a city not far distant from Philippi, learning that Brutus and Cassius had taken their positions in anticipation of an attack, advanced immediately and encamped upon the plain. Octavius was detained by sickness at the city of Dyrrachium, not very far distant. Antony waited for him. It was ten days before he came. At length he arrived, though in coming he had to be borne upon a litter, being still too sick to travel in any other way. Antony approached, and established his camp opposite to that of Cassius, near the sea, while Octavius took post opposite to Brutus. The four armies then paused, contemplating the probable results of the engagement that was about to ensue.

The forces on the two sides were nearly equal; but on the Republican side, that is, on the part of Brutus and Cassius, there was great inconvenience and suffering for want of a sufficient supply of provisions and stores. There was some difference of opinion between Brutus and Cassius in respect to what it was best for them to do. Brutus was inclined to give the enemy battle. Cassius was reluctant to do so, since, under the circumstances in which they were placed, he considered it unwise to hazard, as they necessarily must do, the whole success of their cause to the chances of a single battle. A council of war was convened, and the various officers were asked to give their opinions. In this conference, one of the officers having recommended to postpone the conflict to the next winter, Brutus asked him what advantage he hoped to attain by such delay. "If I gain nothing else," replied the officer, "I shall live so much the longer." This answer touched Cassius's pride and military sense of honor. Rather than concur in a counsel which was thus, on the part of one of its advocates at least, dictated by what he considered an inglorious love of life, he preferred to retract his opinion. It was agreed by the council that the army should maintain its ground and give the enemy battle. The officers then repaired to their respective camps.

Brutus was greatly pleased at this decision. To fight the battle had been his original desire, and as his counsels had prevailed, he was, of course, gratified with the prospect for the morrow. He arranged a sumptuous entertainment in his tent, and invited all the officers of his division of the army to sup with him. The party spent the night in convivial pleasures, and in mutual congratulations at the prospect of the victory which, as they believed, awaited them on the morrow. Brutus entertained his guests with brilliant conversation all the evening, and inspired them with his own confident anticipations of success in the conflict which was to ensue.

Cassius, on the other hand, in his camp by the sea, was silent and desponding. He supped privately with a few intimate friends. On rising from the table, he took one of his officers aside, and, pressing his hand, said to him that he felt great misgivings in respect to the result of the contest. "It is against my judgment," said he, "that we thus hazard the liberty of Rome on the event of one battle, fought under such circumstances as these. Whatever is the result, I wish you to bear me witness hereafter that I was forced into this measure by circumstances that I could not control. I suppose, however, that I ought to take courage, notwithstanding the reasons that I have for these gloomy forebodings. Let us, therefore, hope for the best; and come and sup with me again to-morrow night. To-morrow is my birth-day."

The next morning, the scarlet mantle—the customary signal displayed in Roman camps on the morning of a day of battle—was seen at the tops of the tents of the two commanding generals, waving there in the air like a banner. While the troops, in obedience to this signal, were preparing themselves for the conflict, the two generals went to meet each other at a point midway between their two encampments, for a final consultation and agreement in respect to the arrangements of the day. When this business was concluded, and they were about to separate, in order to proceed each to his own sphere of duty, Cassius asked Brutus what he intended to do in case the day should go against them. "We hope for the best," said he, "and pray that the gods may grant us the victory in this most momentous crisis. But we must remember that it is the greatest and the most momentous of human affairs that are always the most uncertain, and we can not foresee what is to-day to be the result of the battle. If it goes against us, what do you intend to do? Do you intend to escape, or to die?"

"When I was a young man," said Brutus, in reply, "and looked at this subject only as a question of theory, I thought it wrong for a man ever to take his own life. However great the evils that threatened him, and however desperate his condition, I considered it his duty to live, and to wait patiently for better times. But now, placed in the position in which I am, I see the subject in a different light. If we do not gain the battle this day, I shall consider all hope and possibility of saving our country forever gone, and I shall not leave the field of battle alive."

Cassius, in his despondency, had made the same resolution for himself before, and he was rejoiced to hear Brutus utter these sentiments. He grasped his colleague's hand with a countenance expressive of the greatest animation and pleasure, and bade him farewell, saying, "We will go out boldly to face the enemy. For we are certain either that we shall conquer them, or that we shall have nothing to fear from their victory over us."

Cassius's dejection, and the tendency of his mind to take a despairing view of the prospects of the cause in which he was engaged, were owing, in some measure, to certain unfavorable omens which he had observed. These omens, though really frivolous and wholly unworthy of attention, seem to have had great influence upon him, notwithstanding his general intelligence, and the remarkable strength and energy of his character. They were as follows:

In offering certain sacrifices, he was to wear, according to the usage prescribed on such occasions, a garland of flowers, and it happened that the officer who brought the garland, by mistake or accident, presented it wrong side before. Again, in some procession which was formed, and in which a certain image of gold, made in honor of him, was borne, the bearer of it stumbled and fell, and the image was thrown upon the ground. This was a very dark presage of impending calamity. Then a great number of vultures and other birds of prey were seen for a number of days before the battle, hovering over the Roman army; and several swarms of bees were found within the precincts of the camp. So alarming was this last indication, that the officers altered the line of the intrenchments so as to shut out the ill-omened spot from the camp. These and other such things had great influence upon the mind of Cassius, in convincing him that some great disaster was impending over him.

Nor was Brutus himself without warnings of this character, though they seem to have had less power to produce any serious impression upon his mind than in the case of Cassius. The most extraordinary warning which Brutus received, according to the story of his ancient historians, was by a supernatural apparition which he saw, some time before, while he was in Asia Minor. He was encamped near the city of Sardis at that time. He was always accustomed to sleep very little, and would often, it was said, when all his officers had retired, and the camp was still, sit alone in his tent, sometimes reading, and sometimes revolving the anxious cares which were always pressing upon his mind. One night he was thus alone in his tent, with a small lamp burning before him, sitting lost in thought, when he suddenly heard a movement as of some one entering the tent. He looked up, and saw a strange, unearthly, and monstrous shape, which appeared to have just entered the door and was coming toward him. The spirit gazed upon him as it advanced, but it did not speak.

Brutus, who was not much accustomed to fear, boldly demanded of the apparition who and what it was, and what had brought it there. "I am your evil spirit," said the apparition. "I shall meet you at Philippi." "Then, it seems," said Brutus, "that, at any rate, I shall see you again." The spirit made no reply to this, but immediately vanished.

Brutus arose, went to the door of his tent, summoned the sentinels, and awakened the soldiers that were sleeping near. The sentinels had seen nothing; and, after the most diligent search, no trace of the mysterious visitor could be found.

The next morning Brutus related to Cassius the occurrence which he had witnessed. Cassius, though very sensitive, it seems, to the influence of omens affecting himself, was quite philosophical in his views in respect to those of other men. He argued very rationally with Brutus to convince him that the vision which he had seen was only a phantom of sleep, taking its form and character from the ideas and images which the situation in which Brutus was then placed, and the fatigue and anxiety which he had endured, would naturally impress upon his mind.

But to return to the battle. Brutus fought against Octavius; while Cassius, two or three miles distant, encountered Antony, that having been, as will be recollected, the disposition of the respective armies and their encampments upon the plain. Brutus was triumphantly successful in his part of the field. His troops defeated the army of Octavius, and got possession of his camp. The men forced their way into Octavius's tent, and pierced the litter in which they supposed that the sick general was lying through and through with their spears. But the object of their desperate hostility was not there. He had been borne away by his guards a few minutes before, and no one knew what had become of him.

The result of the battle was, however, unfortunately for those whose adventures we are now more particularly following, very different in Cassius's part of the field. When Brutus, after completing the conquest of his own immediate foes, returned to his elevated camp, he looked toward the camp of Cassius, and was surprised to find that the tents had disappeared. Some of the officers around perceived weapons glancing and glittering in the sun in the place where Cassius's tents ought to appear. Brutus now suspected the truth, which was, that Cassius had been defeated, and his camp had fallen into the hands of the enemy. He immediately collected together as large a force as he could command, and marched to the relief of his colleague. He found him, at last, posted with a small body of guards and attendants upon the top of a small elevation to which he had fled for safety. Cassius saw the troop of horsemen which Brutus sent forward coming toward him, and supposed that it was a detachment from Antony's army advancing to capture him. He, however, sent a messenger forward to meet them, and ascertain whether they were friends or foes. The messenger, whose name was Titinius, rode down. The horsemen recognized Titinius, and, riding up eagerly around him, they dismounted from their horses to congratulate him on his safety, and to press him with inquiries in respect to the result of the battle and the fate of his master.

Cassius, seeing all this, but not seeing it very distinctly, supposed that the troop of horsemen were enemies, and that they had surrounded Titinius, and had cut him down or made him prisoner. He considered it certain, therefore, that all was now finally lost. Accordingly, in execution of a plan which he had previously formed, he called a servant, named Pindarus, whom he directed to follow him, and went into a tent which was near. When Brutus and his horsemen came up, they entered the tent. They found no living person within; but the dead body of Cassius was there, the head being totally dissevered from it. Pindarus was never afterward to be found.

Brutus was overwhelmed with grief at the death of his colleague; he was also oppressed by it with a double burden of responsibility and care, since now the whole conduct of affairs devolved upon him alone. He found himself surrounded with difficulties which became more and more embarrassing every day. At length he was compelled to fight a second battle. The details of the contest itself we can not give, but the result of it was, that, notwithstanding the most unparalleled and desperate exertions made by Brutus to keep his men to the work, and to maintain his ground, his troops were borne down and overwhelmed by the irresistible onsets of his enemies, and his cause was irretrievably and hopelessly ruined.

When Brutus found that all was lost, he allowed himself to be conducted off the field by a small body of guards, who, in their retreat, broke through the ranks of the enemy on a side where they saw that they should meet with the least resistance. They were, however, pursued by a squadron of horse, the horsemen being eager to make Brutus a prisoner. In this emergency, one of Brutus's friends, named Lucilius, conceived the design of pretending to be Brutus, and, as such, surrendering himself a prisoner. This plan he carried into effect. When the troop came up, he called out for quarter, said that he was Brutus, and begged them to spare his life, and to take him to Antony. The men did so, rejoiced at having, as they imagined, secured so invaluable a prize.

In the mean time, the real Brutus pressed on to make his escape. He crossed a brook which came in his way, and entered into a little dell, which promised to afford a hiding-place, since it was encumbered with precipitous rocks and shaded with trees. A few friends and officers accompanied Brutus in his flight. Night soon came on, and he lay down in a little recess under a shelving rock, exhausted with fatigue and suffering. Then, raising his eyes to heaven, he imprecated, in lines quoted from a Greek poet, the just judgment of God upon the foes who were at that hour triumphing in what he considered the ruin of his country.

He then, in his anguish and despair, enumerated by name the several friends and companions whom he had seen fall that day in battle, mourning the loss of each with bitter grief. In the mean time, night was coming on, and the party, concealed thus in the wild dell, were destitute and unsheltered. Hungry and thirsty, and spent with fatigue as they were, there seemed to be no prospect for them of either rest or refreshment. Finally they sent one of their number to steal softly back to the rivulet which they had crossed in their retreat, to bring them some water. The soldier took his helmet to bring the water in for want of any other vessel. While Brutus was drinking the water which they brought, a noise was heard in the opposite direction. Two of the officers were sent to ascertain the cause. They came back soon, reporting that there was a party of the enemy in that quarter. They asked where the water was which had been brought. Brutus told them that it had all been drunk, but that he would send immediately for more. The messenger went accordingly to the brook again, but he came back very soon, wounded and bleeding, and reported that the enemy was close upon them on that side too, and that he had narrowly escaped with his life. The apprehensions of Brutus's party were greatly increased by these tidings; it was evident that all hope of being able to remain long concealed where they were must fast disappear.

One of the officers, named Statilius, then proposed to make the attempt to find his way out of the snare in which they had become involved. He would go, he said, as cautiously as possible, avoiding all parties of the enemy, and being favored by the darkness of the night, he hoped to find some way of retreat. If he succeeded, he would display a torch on a distant elevation which he designated, so that the party in the glen, on seeing the light, might be assured of his safety. He would then return and guide them all through the danger, by the way which he should have discovered.

This plan was approved, and Statilius accordingly departed. In due time the light was seen burning at the place which had been pointed out, and indicating that Statilius had accomplished his undertaking. Brutus and his party were greatly cheered by the new hope which this result awakened. They began to watch and listen for their messenger's return. They watched and waited long, but he did not come. On the way back he was intercepted and slain.

When at length all hope that he would return was finally abandoned, some of the party, in the course of the despairing consultations which the unhappy fugitives held with one another, said that they *must not* remain any longer where they were, but must make their escape from that spot at all hazards. "Yes," said Brutus, "we must indeed make our escape from our present situation, but we must do it with our hands, and not with our feet." He meant by this that the only means now left to them to evade their enemies was self-destruction. When his friends understood that this was his meaning, and that he was resolved to put this design into execution in his own case, they were overwhelmed with sorrow. Brutus took them, one by one, by the hand and bade them farewell. He thanked them for their fidelity in adhering to his cause to the last, and said that it was a source of great comfort and satisfaction to him that all his friends had proved so faithful and true. "I do not complain of my hard fate," he added, "so far as I myself am concerned. I mourn only for my unhappy country. As to myself, I think that my condition even now is better than that of my enemies; for though I die, posterity will do me justice, and I shall enjoy forever the honor which virtue and integrity deserve; while they, though they live, live only to reap the bitter fruits of injustice and of tyranny.

"After I am gone," he continued, addressing his friends, as before, "think no longer of me, but take care of yourselves. Antony, I am sure, will be satisfied with Cassius's death and mine. He will not be disposed to pursue you vindictively any longer. Make peace with him on the best terms that you can."

Brutus then asked first one and then another of his friends to aid him in the last duty, as he seems to have considered it, of destroying his life; but one after another declared that they could not do any thing to assist him in carrying into effect so dreadful a determination. Finally, he took with him an old and long-tried friend named Strato, and went away a little, apart from the rest. Here he solicited once more the favor which had been refused him before,—begging that Strato would hold out his sword. Strato still refused. Brutus then called one of his slaves. Upon this Strato declared that he would do any thing rather than that Brutus should die by the hand of a slave. He took the sword, and with his right hand held it extended in the air. With the left hand he covered his eyes, that he might not witness the horrible spectacle. Brutus rushed upon the point of the weapon with such fatal force that he fell and immediately expired.

Thus ended the great and famous battle of Philippi, celebrated in history as marking the termination of the great conflict between the friends and the enemies of Caesar, which agitated the world so deeply after the conqueror's death. This battle established the ascendency of Antony, and made him for a time the most conspicuous man, as Cleopatra was the most conspicuous woman, in the world.

CHAPTER X.

CLEOPATRA AND ANTONY.

Cleopatra espouses Antony's cause.—Her motives.—Antony's early life.—His character.—Personal habits of Antony.—His dress and manners.—Vicious indulgences of Antony.—Public condemnation.—Vices of the great.—Candidates for office.—Antony's excesses.—His luxury and extravagance.—Antony's energy.—His powers of endurance.—Antony's vicissitudes.—He inveighs away the troops of Lepidus.—Antony's marriage.—Fulvia's character.—Fulvia's influence over Antony.—The sudden return.—Change in Antony's character.—His generosity.—Funeral ceremonies of Brutus.—Antony's movements.—Antony's summons to Cleopatra.—The messenger Dellius.—Cleopatra resolves to go to Antony.—Her preparations.—Cleopatra enters the Cydnus.—Her splendid barge.—A scene of enchantment.—Antony's invitation refused. —Cleopatra's reception of Antony.—Antony outdone.—Murder of Arsinoe.—Cleopatra's manner of life at Tarsus.—Cleopatra's munificence.—Story of the pearls.—Position of Fulvia.—Her anxiety and distress.—Antony proposes to go to Rome.—His plans frustrated by Cleopatra.—Antony's infatuation.—Feasting and revelry.—Philotas.—The story of the eight boats.—Antony's son.—The garrulous guest.—The puzzle.—The gold and silver plate returned.—Debasing pleasures. —Antony and Cleopatra in disguise.—Fishing excursions.—Stratagems. —Fulvia's plans for compelling Antony to return.—Departure of Antony.—Chagrin of Cleopatra.

How far Cleopatra was influenced, in her determination to espouse the cause of Antony rather than that of Brutus and Cassius, in the civil war described in the last chapter, by gratitude to Caesar, and how far, on the other hand, by personal interest in Antony, the reader must judge. Cleopatra had seen Antony, it will be recollected, some years before, during his visit to Egypt, when she was a young girl. She was doubtless well acquainted with his character. It was a character peculiarly fitted, in some respects, to captivate the imagination of a woman so ardent, and impulsive, and bold as Cleopatra was fast becoming.

Antony had, in fact, made himself an object of universal interest throughout the world, by his wild and eccentric manners and reckless conduct, and by the very extraordinary vicissitudes which had marked his career. In moral character he was as utterly abandoned and depraved as it was possible to be. In early life, as has already been stated, he plunged into such a course of dissipation and extravagance that he became utterly and hopelessly ruined; or, rather, he would have been so, had he not, by the influence of that magic power of fascination which such characters often possess, succeeded in gaining a great ascendency over a young man of immense fortune, named Curio, who for a time upheld him by becoming surety for his debts. This resource, however, soon failed, and Antony was compelled to abandon Rome, and to live for some years as a fugitive and exile, in dissolute wretchedness and want. During all the subsequent vicissitudes through which he passed in the course of his career, the same habits of lavish expenditure continued, whenever he had funds at his command. This trait of character took the form sometimes of a noble generosity. In his campaigns, the plunder which he acquired he usually divided among his soldiers, reserving nothing for himself. This made his men enthusiastically devoted to him, and led them to consider his prodigality as a virtue, even when they did not themselves derive any direct advantage from it. A thousand stories were always in circulation in camp of acts on his part illustrating his reckless disregard of the value of money, some ludicrous, and all eccentric and strange.

In his personal habits, too, he was as different as possible from other men. He prided himself on being descended from Hercules, and he affected a style of dress and a general air and manner in accordance with the savage character of this his pretended ancestor. His features were sharp, his nose was arched and prominent, and he wore his hair and beard very long—as long, in fact, as he could make them grow. These peculiarities imparted to his countenance a very wild and ferocious expression. He adopted a style of dress, too, which, judged of with reference to the prevailing fashions of the time, gave to his whole appearance a rough, savage, and reckless air. His manner and demeanor corresponded with his dress and appearance. He lived in habits of the most unreserved familiarity with his soldiers. He associated freely with them, ate and drank with them in the open air, and joined in their noisy mirth and rude and boisterous hilarity. His commanding powers of mind, and the desperate recklessness of his courage, enabled him to do all this without danger. These qualities inspired in the minds of the soldiers a feeling of profound respect for their commander; and this good opinion he was enabled to retain, notwithstanding such habits of familiarity with his inferiors as would have been fatal to the influence of an ordinary man.

In the most prosperous portion of Antony's career—for example, during the period immediately preceding the death of Caesar—he addicted himself to vicious indulgences of the most open, public, and shameless character. He had around him a sort of court, formed of jesters, tumblers, mountebanks, play-actors, and other similar characters of the lowest and most disreputable class. Many of these companions were singing and dancing girls, very beautiful, and very highly accomplished in the arts of their respective professions, but all totally corrupt and depraved. Public sentiment, even in that age and nation, strongly condemned this conduct. The people were pagans, it is true, but it is a mistake to suppose that the formation of a moral sentiment in the community against such vices as these is a work which Christianity alone can perform. There is a law of nature, in the form of an instinct universal in the race, imperiously enjoining that the connection of the sexes shall consist of the union of one man with one woman, and that woman his wife, and very sternly prohibiting every other. So that there has probably never been a community in the world so corrupt, that a man could practice in it such vices as those of Antony, without not only violating his own sense of right and wrong, but also bringing upon himself the general condemnation of those around him.

Still, the world is prone to be very tolerant in respect to the vices of the great. Such exalted personages as Antony seem to be judged by a different standard from common men. Even in the countries where those who occupy high stations of trust or of power are actually selected, for the purpose of being placed there, by the voices of their fellow-men, all inquiry into the personal character of a candidate is often suppressed, such inquiry being condemned as wholly irrelevant and improper, and they who succeed in attaining to power enjoy immunities in their elevation which are denied to common men.

But, notwithstanding the influence of Antony's rank and power in shielding him from public censure, he carried his excesses to such an extreme that his conduct was very loudly and very generally condemned. He would spend all the night in carousals, and then, the next day, would appear in public, staggering in the streets. Sometimes he would enter the tribunals for the transaction of business when he was so intoxicated that it would be necessary for friends to come to his assistance to conduct him away. In some of his journeys in the neighborhood of Rome, he would take a troop of companions with him of the worst possible character, and travel with them openly and without shame. There was a certain actress, named Cytheride, whom he made his companion on one such occasion. She was borne upon a litter in his train, and he carried about with him a vast collection of gold and silver plate, and of splendid table furniture, together with an endless supply of luxurious articles of food and of wine, to provide for the entertainments and banquets which he was to celebrate with her on the journey. He would sometimes stop by the road side, pitch his tents, establish his kitchens, set his cooks at work to prepare a feast, spread his tables, and make a sumptuous banquet of the most costly, complete, and ceremonious character—all to make men wonder at the abundance and perfection of the means of luxury which he could carry with him wherever he might go. In fact, he always seemed to feel a special pleasure in doing strange and extraordinary things in order to excite surprise. Once on a journey he had lions harnessed to his carts to draw his baggage, in order to create a sensation.

Notwithstanding the heedlessness with which Antony abandoned himself to these luxurious pleasures when at Rome, no man could endure exposure and hardship better when in camp or on the field. In fact, he rushed with as much headlong precipitation into difficulty and danger when abroad, as into expense and dissipation when at home. During his contests with Octavius and Lepidus, after Caesar's death, he once had occasion to pass the Alps, which, with his customary recklessness, he attempted to traverse without any proper supplies of stores or means of transportation. He was reduced, on the passage, together with the troops under his command, to the most extreme destitution and distress. They had to feed on roots and herbs, and finally on the bark of trees; and they barely preserved themselves, by these means, from actual starvation. Antony seemed, however, to care nothing for all this, but pressed on through the difficulty and danger, manifesting the same daring and determined unconcern to the end. In the same campaign he found himself at one time reduced to extreme destitution in respect to men. His troops had been gradually wasted away until his situation had become very desperate. He conceived, under these circumstances, the most extraordinary idea of going over alone to the camp of Lepidus and enticing away his rival's troops from under the very eyes of their commander. This bold design was successfully executed. Antony advanced alone, clothed in wretched garments, and with his matted hair and beard hanging about his breast and shoulders, up to Lepidus's lines. The men, who knew him well, received him with acclamations; and pitying the sad condition to which they saw that he was reduced, began to listen to what he had to say. Lepidus, who could not attack him, since he and Antony were not at that time in open hostility to each other, but were only rival commanders in the same army, ordered the trumpeters to sound in order to make a noise which should prevent the words of Antony from being heard. This interrupted the negotiation; but the men immediately disguised two of their number in female apparel, and sent them to Antony to make arrangements with him for putting themselves under his command, and offering, at the same time, to murder Lepidus, if he would but speak the word. Antony charged them to do Lepidus no injury. He, however, went over and took possession of the camp, and assumed the command of the army. He treated Lepidus himself, personally, with extreme politeness, and retained him as a subordinate under his command.

Not far from the time of Caesar's death, Antony was married. The name of the lady was Fulvia. She was a widow at the time of her marriage with Antony, and was a woman of very marked and decided character. She had led a wild and irregular life previous to that time, but she conceived a very strong attachment to her new husband and devoted herself to him from the time of her marriage with the most constant fidelity. She soon acquired a very great ascendency over him, and was the means of effecting a very considerable reform in his conduct and character. She was an ambitious and aspiring woman, and made many very efficient and successful efforts to promote the elevation and aggrandizement of her husband. She appeared, also, to take a great pride and pleasure in exercising over him, herself, a great personal control. She succeeded in these attempts in a manner that surprised every body. It seemed astonishing to all mankind that such a tiger as he had been could be subdued by any human power. Nor was it by gentleness and mildness that Fulvia gained such power over her husband. She was of a very stern and masculine character, and she seems to have mastered Antony by surpassing him in the use of his own weapons. In fact, instead of attempting to soothe and mollify him, she reduced him, it seems, to the necessity of resorting to various contrivances to soften and propitiate her. Once, for example, on his return from a campaign in which he had been exposed to great dangers, he disguised himself and came home at night in the garb of a courier bearing dispatches. He caused himself to be ushered, muffled and disguised as he was, into Fulvia's apartments, where he handed her some pretended letters, which, he said, were from her husband; and while Fulvia was opening them in great excitement and trepidation, he threw off his disguise, and revealed himself to her by clasping her in his arms and kissing her in the midst of her amazement.

Antony's marriage with Fulvia, besides being the means of reforming his morals in some degree, softened and civilized him in respect to his manners. His dress and appearance now assumed a different character. In fact, his political elevation after Caesar's death soon became very exalted, and the various democratic arts by which he had sought to raise himself to it, being now no longer necessary, were, as usual in such cases, gradually discarded. He lived in great style and splendor when at Rome, and when absent from home, on his military campaigns, he began to exhibit the same pomp and parade in his equipage and in his arrangements as were usual in the camps of other Roman generals.

After the battle of Philippi, described in the last chapter, Antony—who, with all his faults, was sometimes a very generous foe—as soon as the tidings of Brutus's death were brought to him, repaired immediately to the spot, and appeared to be quite shocked and concerned at the sight of the body. He took off his own military cloak or mantle—which was a very magnificent and costly garment, being enriched with many expensive ornaments—and spread it over the corpse. He then gave directions to one of the officers of his household to make arrangements for funeral ceremonies of a very imposing character, as a testimony of his respect for the memory of the deceased. In these ceremonies it was the duty of the officer to have burned the military cloak which Antony had appropriated to the purpose of a pall, with the body. He did not, however, do so. The cloak being very valuable, he reserved it; and he withheld, also, a considerable part of the money which had been given him for the expenses of the funeral. He supposed that Antony would probably not inquire very closely into the details of the arrangements made for the funeral of his most inveterate enemy. Antony, however, did inquire into them, and when he learned what the officer had done, he ordered him to be killed.

The various political changes which occurred, and the movements which took place among the several armies after the battle of Philippi, can not be here detailed. It is sufficient to say that Antony proceeded to the eastward through Asia Minor, and in the course of the following year came into Cilicia. From this place he sent a messenger to Egypt to Cleopatra, summoning her to appear before him. There were charges, he said, against her of having aided Cassius and Brutus in the late war instead of rendering assistance to him. Whether there really were any such charges, or whether they were only fabricated by Antony as pretexts for seeing Cleopatra, the fame of whose beauty was very widely extended, does not certainly appear. However this may be, he sent to summon the queen to come to him. The name of the messenger whom Antony dispatched on this errand was Dellius. Fulvia, Antony's wife, was not with him at this time. She had been left behind at Rome.

Dellius proceeded to Egypt and appeared at Cleopatra's court. The queen was at this time about twenty-eight, but more beautiful, as was said, than ever before. Dellius was very much struck with her beauty and with a certain fascination in her voice and conversation, of which her ancient biographers often speak as one of the most irresistible of her charms. He told her that she need have no fear of Antony. It was of no consequence, he said, what charges there might be against her. She would find that, in a very few days after she had entered into Antony's presence, she would be in great favor. She might rely, in fact, he said, on gaining, very speedily, an unbounded ascendency over the general. He advised her, therefore, to proceed to Cilicia without fear; and to present herself before Antony in as much pomp and magnificence as she could command. He would answer, he said, for the result.

Cleopatra determined to follow this advice. In fact, her ardent and impulsive imagination was fired with the idea of making, a second time, the conquest of the greatest general and highest potentate in the world. She began immediately to make provision for the voyage. She employed all the resources of her kingdom in procuring for herself the most magnificent means of display, such as expensive and splendid dresses, rich services of plate, ornaments of precious stones and of gold, and presents in great variety and of the most costly description for Antony. She appointed, also, a numerous retinue of attendants to accompany her, and, in a word, made all the arrangements complete for an expedition of the most imposing and magnificent character. While these preparations were going forward, she received new and frequent communications from Antony, urging her to hasten her departure; but she paid very little attention to them. It was evident that she felt quite independent, and was intending to take her own time.

At length, however, all was ready, and Cleopatra set sail. She crossed the Mediterranean Sea, and entered the mouth of the River Cydnus. Antony was at Tarsus, a city upon the Cydnus, a small distance above its mouth. When Cleopatra's fleet had entered the river, she embarked on board a most magnificent barge which she had constructed for the occasion, and had brought with her across the sea. This barge was the most magnificent and highly-ornamented vessel that had ever been built. It was adorned with carvings and decorations of the finest workmanship, and elaborately gilded. The sails were of purple, and the oars were inlaid and tipped with silver. Upon the deck of this barge Queen Cleopatra appeared, under a canopy of cloth of gold. She was dressed very magnificently in the costume in which Venus, the goddess of Beauty, was then generally represented. She was surrounded by a company of beautiful boys, who attended upon her in the form of Cupids, and fanned her with their wings, and by a group of young girls representing the Nymphs and the Graces. There was a band of musicians stationed upon the deck. This music guided the oarsmen, as they kept time to it in their rowing; and, soft as the melody was, the strains were heard far and wide over the water and along the shores, as the beautiful vessel advanced on its way. The performers were provided with flutes, lyres, viols, and all the other instruments customarily used in those times to produce music of a gentle and voluptuous kind.

[Illustration: MEETING OF CLEOPATRA AND ANTONY.]

In fact, the whole spectacle seemed like a vision of enchantment. Tidings of the approach of the barge spread rapidly around, and the people of the country came down in crowds to the shores of the river to gaze upon it in admiration as it glided slowly along. At the time of its arrival at Tarsus, Antony was engaged in giving a public audience at some tribunal in his palace, but everybody ran to see Cleopatra and the barge, and the great triumvir was left consequently alone, or, at least, with only a few official attendants near him. Cleopatra, on arriving at the city, landed, and began to pitch her tents on the shores. Antony sent a messenger to bid her welcome, and to invite her to come and sup with him. She declined the invitation, saying that it was more proper that he should come and sup with her. She would accordingly expect him to come, she said, and her tents would be ready at the proper hour. Antony complied with her proposal, and came to her entertainment. He was received with a magnificence and splendor which amazed him. The tents and pavilions where the entertainment was made were illuminated with an immense number of lamps. These lamps were arranged in a very ingenious and beautiful manner, so as to produce an illumination of the most surprising brilliancy and beauty. The immense number and variety, too, of the meats and wines, and of the vessels of gold and silver, with which the tables were loaded, and the magnificence and splendor of the dresses worn by Cleopatra and her attendants, combined to render the whole scene one of bewildering enchantment.

The next day, Antony invited Cleopatra to come and return his visit; but, though he made every possible effort to provide a banquet as sumptuous and as sumptuously served as hers, he failed entirely in this attempt, and acknowledged himself completely outdone. Antony was, moreover, at these interviews, perfectly fascinated with Cleopatra's charms. Her beauty, her wit, her thousand accomplishments, and, above all, the tact, and adroitness, and self-possession which she displayed in assuming at once so boldly, and carrying out so adroitly, the idea of her social superiority over him, that he yielded his heart almost immediately to her undisputed sway.

The first use which Cleopatra made of her power was to ask Antony, for her sake, to order her sister Arsinoe to be slain. Arsinoe had gone, it will be recollected, to Rome, to grace Caesar's triumph there, and had afterward retired to Asia, where she was now living an exile. Cleopatra, either from a sentiment of past revenge, or else from some apprehensions of future danger, now desired that her sister should die. Antony readily acceded to her request. He sent an officer in search of the unhappy princess. The officer slew her where he found her, within the precincts of a temple to which she had fled, supposing it a sanctuary which no degree of hostility, however extreme, would have dared to violate.

Cleopatra remained at Tarsus for some time, revolving in an incessant round of gayety and pleasure, and living in habits of unrestrained intimacy with Antony. She was accustomed to spend whole days and nights with him in feasting and revelry. The immense magnificence of these entertainments, especially on Cleopatra's part, were the wonder of the world. She seems to have taken special pleasure in exciting Antony's surprise by the display of her wealth and the boundless extravagance in which she indulged. At one of her banquets, Antony was expressing his astonishment at the vast number of gold cups, enriched with jewels, that were displayed on all sides. "Oh," said she, "they are nothing; if you like them, you shall have them all." So saying, she ordered her servants to carry them to Antony's house. The next day she invited Antony again, with a large number of the chief officers of his army and court. The table was spread with a new service of gold and silver vessels, more extensive and splendid than that of the preceding day; and at the close of the supper, when the company was about to depart, Cleopatra distributed all these treasures among the guests that had been present at the entertainment. At another of these feasts, she carried her ostentation and display to the astonishing extreme of taking off from one of her ear-rings a pearl of immense value and dissolving it in a cup of vinegar,[1] which she afterward made into a drink, such as was customarily used in those days, and then drank it. She was proceeding to do the same with the other pearl, when some of the company arrested the proceeding, and took the remaining pearl away.

[Footnote 1: Pearls, being of the nature of *shell* in their composition and structure, are soluble in certain acids.]

In the mean time, while Antony was thus wasting his time in luxury and pleasure with Cleopatra, his public duties were neglected, and every thing was getting into confusion. Fulvia remained in Italy. Her position and her character gave her a commanding political influence, and she exerted herself in a very energetic manner to sustain, in that quarter of the world, the interests of her husband's cause. She was surrounded with difficulties and dangers, the details of which can not, however, be here particularly described. She wrote continually to Antony, urgently entreating him to come to Rome, and displaying in her letters all those marks of agitation and distress which a wife would naturally feel under the circumstances in which she was placed. The thought that her husband had been so completely drawn away from her by the guilty arts of such a woman, and led by her to abandon his wife and his family, and leave in neglect and confusion concerns of such momentous magnitude as those which demanded his attention at home, produced an excitement in her mind bordering upon frensy. Antony was at length so far influenced by the urgency of the case that he determined to return. He broke up his quarters at Tarsus and moved south toward Tyre, which was a great naval port and station in those days. Cleopatra went with him. They were to separate at Tyre. She was to embark there for Egypt, and he for Rome.

At least that was Antony's plan, but it was not Cleopatra's. She had determined that Antony should go with her to Alexandria. As might have been expected, when the time came for the decision, the woman gained the day. Her flatteries, her arts, her caresses, her tears, prevailed. After a brief struggle between the sentiment of love on the one hand and those of ambition and of duty combined on the other, Antony gave up the contest. Abandoning every thing else, he surrendered himself wholly to Cleopatra's control, and went with her to Alexandria. He spent the winter there, giving himself up with her to every species of sensual indulgence that the most remorseless license could tolerate, and the most unbounded wealth procure.

There seemed, in fact, to be no bounds to the extravagance and infatuation which Antony displayed during the winter in Alexandria. Cleopatra devoted herself to him incessantly, day and night, filling up every moment of time with some new form of pleasure, in order that he might have no time to think of his absent wife, or to listen to the reproaches of his conscience. Antony, on his part, surrendered himself a willing victim to these wiles, and entered with all his heart into the thousand plans of gayety and merry-making which Cleopatra devised. They had each a separate establishment in the city, which was maintained at an enormous cost, and they made a regular arrangement by which each was the guest of the other on alternate days. These visits were spent in games, sports, spectacles, feasting, drinking, and in every species of riot, irregularity, and excess.

A curious instance is afforded of the accidental manner in which intelligence in respect to the scenes and incidents of private life in those ancient days is sometimes obtained, in a circumstance which occurred at this time at Antony's court. It seems that there was a young medical student at Alexandria that winter, named Philotas, who happened, in some way or other, to have formed an acquaintance with one of Antony's domestics, a cook. Under the guidance of this cook, Philotas went one day into the palace to see what was to be seen. The cook took his friend into the kitchens, where, to Philotas's great surprise, he saw, among an infinite number and variety of other preparations, eight wild boars roasting before the fires, some being more and some less advanced in the process. Philotas asked what great company was to dine there that day. The cook smiled at this question, and replied that there was to be no company at all, other than Antony's ordinary party. "But," said the cook, in explanation, "we are obliged always to prepare several suppers, and to have them ready in succession at different hours, for no one can tell at what time they will order the entertainment to be served. Sometimes, when the supper has been actually carried in, Antony and Cleopatra will get engaged in some new turn of their diversions, and conclude not to sit down just then to the table, and so we have to take the supper away, and presently bring in another."

Antony had a son with him at Alexandria at this time, the child of his wife Fulvia. The name of the son, as well as that of the father, was Antony. He was old enough to feel some sense of shame at his father's dereliction from duty, and to manifest some respectful regard for the rights and the honor of his mother. Instead of this, however, he imitated his father's example, and, in his own way, was as reckless and extravagant as he. The same Philotas who is above referred to was, after a time, appointed to some office or other in the young Antony's household, so that he was accustomed to sit at his table and share in his convivial enjoyments. He relates that once, while they were feasting together, there was a guest present, a physician, who was a very vain and conceited man, and so talkative that no one else had any opportunity to speak. All the pleasure of conversation was spoiled by his excessive garrulity. Philotas, however, at length puzzled him so completely with a question of logic,—of a kind similar to those often discussed with great interest in ancient days,—as to silence him for a time; and young Antony was so much delighted with this feat, that he gave Philotas all the gold and silver plate that there was upon the table, and sent all the articles home to him, after the entertainment was over, telling him to put his mark and stamp upon them, and lock them up.

The question with which Philotas puzzled the self-conceited physician was this. It must be premised, however, that in those days it was considered that cold water in an intermittent fever was extremely dangerous, except in some peculiar cases, and in those the effect was good. Philotas then argued as follows: "In cases of a certain kind it is best to give water to a patient in an ague. All cases of ague are cases of a certain kind. Therefore it is best in all cases to give the patient water." Philotas having propounded his argument in this way, challenged the physician to point out the fallacy of it; and while the physician sat perplexed and puzzled in his attempts to unravel the intricacy of it, the company enjoyed a temporary respite from his excessive loquacity.

Philotas adds, in his account of this affair, that he sent the gold and silver plate back to young Antony again, being afraid to keep them. Antony said that perhaps it was as well that this should be done, since many of the vessels were of great value on account of their rare and antique workmanship, and his father might possibly miss them and wish to know what had become of them.

As there were no limits, on the one hand, to the loftiness and grandeur of the pleasures to which Antony and Cleopatra addicted themselves, so there were none to the low and debasing tendencies which characterized them on the other. Sometimes, at midnight, after having been spending many hours in mirth and revelry in the palace, Antony would disguise himself in the dress of a slave, and sally forth into the streets, excited with wine, in search of adventures. In many cases, Cleopatra herself, similarly disguised, would go out with him. On these excursions Antony would take pleasure in involving himself in all sorts of difficulties and dangers—in street riots, drunken brawls, and desperate quarrels with the populace—all for Cleopatra's amusement and his own. Stories of these adventures would circulate afterward among the people, some of whom would admire the free and jovial character of their eccentric visitor, and others would despise him as a prince degrading himself to the level of a brute.

Some of the amusements and pleasures which Antony and Cleopatra pursued were innocent in themselves, though wholly unworthy to be made the serious business of life by personages on whom such exalted duties rightfully devolved. They made various excursions upon the Nile, and arranged parties of pleasure to go out on the water in the harbor, and to various rural retreats in the environs of the city. Once they went out on a fishing-party, in boats, in the port. Antony was unsuccessful; and feeling chagrined that Cleopatra should witness his ill-luck, he made a secret arrangement with some of the fishermen to dive down, where they could do so unobserved, and fasten fishes to his hook under the water. By this plan he caught very large and fine fish very fast. Cleopatra, however, was too wary to be easily deceived by such a stratagem as this. She observed the maneuver, but pretended not to observe it; she expressed, on the other hand, the greatest surprise and delight at Antony's good luck, and the extraordinary skill which it indicated.

The next day she wished to go a fishing again, and a party was accordingly made as on the day before. She had, however, secretly instructed another fisherman to procure a dried and salted fish from the market, and, watching his opportunity, to get down into the water under the boats and attach it to the hook, before Antony's divers could get there. This plan succeeded, and Antony, in the midst of a large and gay party that were looking on, pulled out an excellent fish, cured and dried, such as was known to every one as an imported article, bought in the market. It was a fish of a kind that was brought originally from Asia Minor. The boats and the water all around them resounded with the shouts of merriment and laughter which this incident occasioned.

In the mean time, while Antony was thus spending his time in low and ignoble pursuits and in guilty pleasures at Alexandria, his wife Fulvia, after exhausting all other means of inducing her husband to return to her, became desperate, and took measures for fomenting an open war, which she thought would compel him to return. The extraordinary energy, influence, and talent which Fulvia possessed, enabled her to do this in an effectual manner. She organized an army, formed a camp, placed herself at the head of the troops, and sent such tidings to Antony of the dangers which threatened his cause as greatly alarmed him. At the same time news came of great disasters in Asia Minor, and of alarming insurrections among the provinces which had been committed to his charge there. Antony saw that he must arouse himself from the spell which had enchanted him and break away from Cleopatra, or that he would be wholly and irretrievably ruined. He made, accordingly, a desperate effort to get free. He bade the queen farewell, embarked hastily in a fleet of galleys, and sailed away to Tyre, leaving Cleopatra in her palace, vexed, disappointed, and chagrined.

CHAPTER XI.

THE BATTLE OF ACTIUM.

Perplexity of Antony.—His meeting with Fulvia.—Meeting of Antony and Fulvia.—Reconciliation of Antony and Octavius.—Octavia.—Her marriage to Antony.—Octavia's influence over her husband and her brother.—Octavia pleads for Antony.—Difficulties settled.—Antony tired of his wife.—He goes to Egypt.—Antony again with Cleopatra.—Effect on his character.—The march to Sidon.—Suffering of the troops.—Arrival of Cleopatra.—She brings supplies for the army.—Octavia intercedes for Antony.—She brings him re-enforcements. —Cleopatra's alarm.—Her arts.—Cleopatra's secret agents.—Their representations to Antony.—Cleopatra's success.—Antony's message to Octavia.—Devotion of Octavia.—Indignation against Antony.—Measures of Antony.—Accusations against him.—Antony's preparations.—Assistance of Cleopatra.—Canidius bribed.—His advice in regard to Cleopatra.—The fleet at Samos.—Antony's infatuation.—Riot and revelry.—Antony and Cleopatra at Athens.—Ostentation of Cleopatra.—Honors bestowed on her.—Baseness of Antony.—Approach of Octavius.—Antony's will.—Charges against him. —Antony's neglect of his duties.—Meeting of the fleets. —Opinions of the council.—Cleopatra's wishes.—Battle of Actium.—Flight of Cleopatra.— Antony follows Cleopatra.—He gains her galley.—Antony pursued.—A severe conflict.—The avenger of a father.—Antony's anguish—Antony and Cleopatra shun each other.—Arrival at Tsenarus.—Antony and Cleopatra fly together to Egypt.

Cleopatra, in parting with Antony as described in the last chapter, lost him for two or three years. During this time Antony himself was involved in a great variety of difficulties and dangers, and passed through many eventful scenes, which, however, can not here be described in detail. His life, during this period, was full of vicissitude and excitement, and was spent probably in alternations of remorse for the past and anxiety for the future. On landing at Tyre, he was at first extremely perplexed whether to go to Asia Minor or to

Rome. His presence was imperiously demanded in both places. The war which Fulvia had fomented was caused, in part, by the rivalry of Octavius, and the collision of his interests with those of her husband. Antony was very angry with her for having managed his affairs in such a way as to bring about a war. After a time Antony and Fulvia met at Athens. Fulvia had retreated to that city, and was very seriously sick there, either from bodily disease, or from the influence of long-continued anxiety, vexation, and distress. They had a stormy meeting. Neither party was disposed to exercise any mercy toward the other. Antony left his wife rudely and roughly, after loading her with reproaches. A short time afterward, she sank down in sorrow to the grave.

The death of Fulvia was an event which proved to be of advantage to Antony. It opened the way to a reconciliation between him and Octavius. Fulvia had been extremely active in opposing Octavius's designs, and in organizing plans for resisting him. He felt, therefore, a special hostility against her, and, through her, against Antony. Now, however, that she was dead, the way seemed to be in some sense opened for a reconciliation.

Octavius had a sister, Octavia, who had been the wife of a Roman general named Marcellus. She was a very beautiful and a very accomplished woman, and of a spirit very different from that of Fulvia. She was gentle, affectionate, and kind, a lover of peace and harmony, and not at all disposed, like Fulvia, to assert and maintain her influence over others by an overbearing and violent demeanor. Octavia's husband died about this time, and, in the course of the movements and negotiations between Antony and Octavius, the plan was proposed of a marriage between Antony and Octavia, which, it was thought, would ratify and confirm the reconciliation. This proposal was finally agreed upon. Antony was glad to find so easy a mode of settling his difficulties. The people of Rome, too, and the authorities there, knowing that the peace of the world depended upon the terms on which these two men stood with regard to each other, were extremely desirous that this arrangement should be carried into effect. There was a law of the commonwealth forbidding the marriage of a widow within a specified period after the death of her husband. That period had not, in Octavia's case, yet expired. There was, however, so strong a desire that no obstacle should be allowed to prevent this proposed union, or even to occasion delay, that the law was altered expressly for this case, and Antony and Octavia were married. The empire was divided between Octavius and Antony, Octavius receiving the western portion as his share, while the eastern was assigned to Antony.

It is not probable that Antony felt any very strong affection for his new wife, beautiful and gentle as she was. A man, in fact, who had led such a life as his had been, must have become by this time incapable of any strong and pure attachment. He, however, was pleased with the novelty of his acquisition, and seemed to forget for a time the loss of Cleopatra. He remained with Octavia a year. After that he went away on certain military enterprises which kept him some time from her. He returned again, and again he went away. All this time Octavia's influence over him and over her brother was of the most salutary and excellent character. She soothed their animosities, quieted their suspicions and jealousies, and at one time, when they were on the brink of open war, she effected a reconciliation between them by the most courageous and energetic, and at the same time, gentle and unassuming efforts. At the time of this danger she was with her husband in Greece; but she persuaded him to send her to her brother at Rome, saying that she was confident that she could arrange a settlement of the difficulties impending. Antony allowed her to go. She proceeded to Rome, and procured an interview with her brother in the presence of his two principal officers of state. Here she pleaded her husband's cause with tears in her eyes; she defended his conduct, explained what seemed to be against him, and entreated her brother not to take such a course as should cast her down from being the happiest of women to being the most miserable. "Consider the circumstances of my case," said she. "The eyes of the world are upon me. Of the two most powerful men in the world, I am the wife of one and the sister of another. If you allow rash counsels to go on and war to ensue, I am hopelessly ruined; for, whichever is conquered, my husband or my brother, my own happiness will be for ever gone."

Octavius sincerely loved his sister, and he was so far softened by her entreaties that he consented to appoint an interview with Antony in order to see if their difficulties could be settled. This interview was accordingly held. The two generals came to a river, where, at the opposite banks, each embarked in a boat, and, being rowed out toward each other, they met in the middle of the stream. A conference ensued, at which all the questions at issue were, for a time at least, very happily arranged.

Antony, however, after a time, began to become tired of his wife, and to sigh for Cleopatra once more. He left Octavia at Rome and proceeded to the eastward, under pretense of attending to the affairs of that portion of the empire; but, instead of doing this, he went to Alexandria, and there renewed again his former intimacy with the Egyptian queen.

Octavius was very indignant at this. His former hostility to Antony, which had been in a measure appeased by the kind influence of Octavia, now broke forth anew, and was heightened by the feeling of resentment naturally awakened by his sister's wrongs Public sentiment in Rome, too, was setting very strongly against Antony. Lampoons were written, against him to ridicule him and Cleopatra, and the most decided censures were passed upon his conduct.

Octavia was universally beloved, and the sympathy which was every where felt for her increased and heightened very much the popular indignation which was felt against the man who could wrong so deeply such sweetness, and gentleness, and affectionate fidelity as hers.

After remaining for some time in Alexandria, and renewing his connection and intimacy with Cleopatra, Antony went away again, crossing the sea into Asia, with the intention of prosecuting certain military undertakings there which imperiously demanded his attention. His plan was to return as soon as possible to Egypt after the object of his expedition should be accomplished. He found, however, that he could not bear even a temporary absence from Cleopatra. His mind dwelled so much upon her, and upon the pleasures which he had enjoyed with her in Egypt, and he longed so much to see her again, that he was wholly unfit for the discharge of his duties in the camp. He became timid, inefficient, and remiss, and almost every thing that he undertook ended disastrously. The army, who understood perfectly well the reason of their commander's remissness and consequent ill fortune, were extremely indignant at his conduct, and the camp was filled with suppressed murmurs and complaints. Antony, however, like other persons in his situation, was blind to all these indications of dissatisfaction; probably he would have disregarded them if he had observed them. At length, finding that he could bear his absence from his mistress no longer, he set out to march across the country, in the depth of the winter, to the sea-shore, to a point where he had sent for Cleopatra to come to join him. The army endured incredible hardships and exposures in this march. When Antony had once commenced the journey, he was so impatient to get forward that he compelled his troops to advance with a rapidity greater than their strength would bear. They were, besides, not provided with proper tents or with proper supplies of provisions. They were often obliged, therefore, after a long and fatiguing march during the day, to bivouac at night in the open air among the mountains, with scanty means of appeasing their hunger, and very little shelter from the cold rain, or from the storms of driving snow. Eight thousand men died on this march, from cold, fatigue, and exposure; a greater sacrifice, perhaps, than had ever been made before to the mere ardor and impatience of a lover.

When Antony reached the shore, he advanced to a certain sea-port, near Sidon, where Cleopatra was to land. At the time of his arrival but a very small part of his army was left, and the few men that survived were in a miserably destitute condition. Antony's eagerness to see Cleopatra became more and more excited as the time drew nigh. She did not come so soon as he had expected, and during the delay he seemed to pine away under the influence of love and sorrow. He was silent, absent-minded, and sad. He had no thoughts for any thing but the coming of Cleopatra, and felt no interest in any other

106

plans. He watched for her incessantly, and would sometimes leave his place at the table, in the midst of the supper, and go down alone to the shore, where he would stand gazing out upon the sea, and saying mournfully to himself, "Why does not she come?" The animosity and the ridicule which these things awakened against him, on the part of the army, were extreme; but he was so utterly infatuated that he disregarded all the manifestations of public sentiment around him, and continued to allow his mind to be wholly engrossed with the single idea of Cleopatra's coming.

She arrived at last. She brought a great supply of clothes and other necessaries for the use of Antony's army, so that her coming not only gratified his love, but afforded him, also, a very essential relief, in respect to the military difficulties in which he was involved.

After some time spent in the enjoyment of the pleasure which being thus reunited to Cleopatra afforded him, Antony began again to think of the affairs of his government, which every month more and more imperiously demanded his attention. He began to receive urgent calls from various quarters, rousing him to action. In the mean time, Octavia—who had been all this while waiting in distress and anxiety at Rome, hearing continually the most gloomy accounts of her husband's affairs, and the most humiliating tidings in respect to his infatuated devotion to Cleopatra—resolved to make one more effort to save him. She interceded with her brother to allow her to raise troops and to collect supplies, and then proceed to the eastward to re-enforce him. Octavius consented to this. He, in fact, assisted Octavia in making her preparations. It is said, however, that he was influenced in this plan by his confident belief that this noble attempt of his sister to reclaim her husband would fail, and that, by the failure of it, Antony would be put in the wrong, in the estimation of the Roman people, more absolutely and hopelessly than ever, and that the way would thus be prepared for his complete and final destruction.

Octavia was rejoiced to obtain her brother's aid to her undertaking, whatever the motive might be which induced him to afford it. She accordingly levied a considerable body of troops, raised a large sum of money, provided clothes, and tents, and military stores for the army; and when all was ready, she left Italy and put to sea, having previously dispatched a messenger to her husband to inform him that she was coming.

Cleopatra began now to be afraid that she was to lose Antony again, and she at once began to resort to the usual artifices employed in such cases, in order to retain her power over him. She said nothing, but assumed the appearance of one pining under the influence of some secret suffering or sorrow. She contrived to be often surprised in tears. In such cases she would hastily brush her tears away, and assume a countenance of smiles and good humor, as if making every effort to be happy, though really oppressed with a heavy burden of anxiety and grief. When Antony was near her she would seem overjoyed at his presence, and gaze upon him with an expression of the most devoted fondness. When absent from him, she spent her time alone, always silent and dejected, and often in tears; and she took care that the secret sorrows and sufferings that she endured should be duly made known to Antony, and that he should understand that they were all occasioned by her love for him, and by the danger which she apprehended that he was about to leave her.

The friends and secret agents of Cleopatra, who reported these things to Antony, made, moreover, direct representations to him, for the purpose of inclining his mind in her favor. They had, in fact, the astonishing audacity to argue that Cleopatra's claims upon Antony for a continuance of his love were paramount to those of Octavia. She, that is, Octavia, had been his wife, they said, only for a very short time. Cleopatra had been most devotedly attached to him for many years. Octavia was married to him, they alleged, not under the impulse of love, but from political considerations alone, to please her brother, and to ratify and confirm a political league made with him. Cleopatra, on the other hand, had given herself up to him in the most absolute and unconditional manner, under the influence solely of a personal affection which she could not control. She had surrendered and sacrificed every thing to him. For him she had lost her good name, alienated the affections of her subjects, made herself the object of reproach and censure to all mankind, and now she had left her native land to come and join him in his adverse fortunes. Considering how much she had done, and suffered, and sacrificed for his sake, it would be extreme and unjustifiable cruelty in him to forsake her now. She never would survive such an abandonment. Her whole soul was so wrapped up in him, that she would pine away and die if he were now to forsake her.

Antony was distressed and agitated beyond measure by the entanglements in which he found that he was involved. His duty, his inclination perhaps, certainly his ambition, and every dictate of prudence and policy required that he should break away from these snares at once and go to meet Octavia. But the spell that bound him was too mighty to be dissolved. He yielded to Cleopatra's sorrows and tears. He dispatched a messenger to Octavia, who had by this time reached Athens, in Greece, directing her not to come any farther. Octavia, who seemed incapable of resentment or anger against her husband, sent back to ask what she should do with the troops, and money, and the military stores which she was bringing. Antony directed her to leave them in Greece. Octavia did so, and mournfully returned to her home.

As soon as she arrived at Rome, Octavius, her brother, whose indignation was now thoroughly aroused at the baseness of Antony, sent to his sister to say that she must leave Antony's house and come to him. A proper self-respect, he said, forbade her remaining any longer under the roof of such a man. Octavia replied that she would not leave her husband's house. That house was her post of duty, whatever her husband might do, and there she would remain. She accordingly retired within the precincts of her old home, and devoted herself in patient and uncomplaining sorrow to the care of the family and the children. Among these children was one young son of Antony's, born during his marriage with her predecessor Fulvia. In the mean time, while Octavia was thus faithfully though mournfully fulfilling her duties as wife and mother, in her husband's house at Rome, Antony himself had gone with Cleopatra to Alexandria, and was abandoning himself once more to a life of guilty pleasure there. The greatness of mind which this beautiful and devoted wife thus displayed, attracted the admiration of all mankind. It produced, however, one other effect, which Octavia must have greatly deprecated. It aroused a strong and universal feeling of indignation against the unworthy object toward whom this extraordinary magnanimity was displayed.

In the mean time, Antony gave himself up wholly to Cleopatra's influence and control, and managed all the affairs of the Roman empire in the East in the way best fitted to promote her aggrandizement and honor. He made Alexandria his capital, celebrated triumphs there, arranged ostentatious expeditions into Asia and Syria with Cleopatra and her train, gave her whole provinces as presents, and exalted her two sons, Alexander and Ptolemy, children born during the period of his first acquaintance with her, to positions of the highest rank and station, as his own acknowledged sons. The consequences of these and similar measures at Rome were fatal to Antony's character and standing. Octavius reported every thing to the Roman Senate and people, and made Antony's misgovernment and his various misdemeanors the ground of the heaviest accusations against him. Antony, hearing of these things, sent his agents to Rome and made accusations against Octavius; but these counter accusations were of no avail. Public sentiment was very strong and decided against him at the capital, and Octavius began to prepare for war.

Antony perceived that he must prepare to defend himself. Cleopatra entered into the plans which he formed for this purpose with great ardor. Antony began to levy troops, and collect and equip galleys and ships of war, and to make requisitions of money and military stores from all the eastern provinces and kingdoms. Cleopatra put all the resources of Egypt at his disposal. She furnished him with immense sums of money, and with an inexhaustible supply of corn, which she procured for this purpose from her dominions in the valley of the Nile. The various divisions of the immense armament which was thus provided for were ordered to rendezvous at Ephesus, where Antony and Cleopatra were awaiting to receive them, having proceeded there when their arrangements in Egypt were completed, and they were ready to commence the campaign.

When all was ready for the expedition to set sail from Ephesus, it was Antony's judgment that it would be best for Cleopatra to return to Egypt, and leave him to go forth with the fleet to meet Octavius alone. Cleopatra was, however, determined not to go away. She did not dare to leave Antony at all to himself, for fear that in some way or other a peace would be effected between himself and Octavius, which would result in his returning to Octavia and abandoning *her*. She accordingly contrived to persuade Antony to retain her with him, by bribing his chief counselor to advise him to do so. His counselor's name was Canidius. Canidius, having received Cleopatra's money, while yet he pretended to be wholly disinterested in his advice, represented to Antony that it would not be reasonable to send Cleopatra away, and deprive her of all participation in the glory of the war, when she was defraying so large a part of the expense of it. Besides, a large portion of the army consisted of Egyptian troops, who would feel discouraged and disheartened if Cleopatra were to leave them, and would probably act far less efficiently in the conflict than they would do if animated by the presence of their queen. Then, moreover, such a woman as Cleopatra was not to be considered, as many women would be, an embarrassment and a source of care to a military expedition which she might join, but a very efficient counselor and aid to it. She was, he said, a very sagacious, energetic, and powerful queen, accustomed to the command of armies and to the management of affairs of state, and her aid in the conduct of the expedition might be expected to conduce very materially to its success.

Antony was easily won by such persuasions as these, and it was at length decided that Cleopatra should accompany him.

Antony then ordered the fleet to move forward to the island of Samos. Here it was brought to anchor and remained for some time, waiting for the coming in of new re-enforcements, and for the completion of the other arrangements. Antony, as if becoming more and more infatuated as he approached the brink of his ruin, spent his time while the expedition remained at Samos, not in maturing his plans and perfecting his arrangements for the tremendous conflict which was approaching, but in festivities, games, revelings, and every species of riot and dissolute excess. This, however, is not surprising. Men almost always, when in a situation analogous to his, fly to similar means of protecting themselves, in some small degree, from the pangs of remorse, and from the forebodings which stand ready to terrify and torment them at every instant in which these gloomy specters are not driven away by intoxication and revelry. At least Antony found it so. Accordingly, an immense company of players, tumblers, fools, jesters, and mountebanks were ordered to assemble at Samos, and to devote themselves with all zeal to the amusement of Antony's court. The island was one universal scene of riot and revelry. People were astonished at such celebrations and displays, wholly unsuitable, as they considered them, to the occasion. If such are the rejoicings, said they, which Antony celebrates before going into the battle, what festivities will he contrive on his return, joyous enough to express his pleasure if he shall gain the victory?

After a time, Antony and Cleopatra, with a magnificent train of attendants, left Samos, and, passing across the Aegean Sea, landed in Greece, and advanced to Athens, while the fleet, proceeding westward from Samos, passed around Taenarus, the southern promontory of Greece, and then moved northward along the western coast of the peninsula. Cleopatra wished to go to Athens for a special reason. It was there that Octavia had stopped on her journey toward her husband with re-enforcements and aid; and while she was there, the people of Athens, pitying her sad condition, and admiring the noble spirit of mind which she displayed in her misfortunes, had paid her great attention, and during her stay among them had bestowed upon her many honors. Cleopatra now wished to go to the same place, and to triumph over her rival there, by making so great a display of her wealth and magnificence, and of her ascendency over the mind of Antony, as should entirely transcend and outshine the more unassuming pretensions of Octavia. She was not willing, it seems, to leave to the unhappy wife whom she had so cruelly wronged even the possession of a place in the hearts of the people of this foreign city, but must go and enviously strive to efface the impression which injured innocence had made, by an ostentatious exhibition of the triumphant prosperity of her own shameless wickedness. She succeeded well in her plans. The people of Athens were amazed and bewildered at the immense magnificence that Cleopatra exhibited before them. She distributed vast sums of money among the people. The city, in return, decreed to her the most exalted honors. They sent a solemn embassy to her to present her with these decrees. Antony himself, in the character of a citizen of Athens, was one of the embassadors. Cleopatra received the deputation at her palace. The reception was attended with the most splendid and imposing ceremonies.

One would have supposed that Cleopatra's cruel and unnatural hostility to Octavia might now have been satisfied; but it was not. Antony, while he was at Athens, and doubtless at Cleopatra's instigation, sent a messenger to Rome with a notice of divorcement to Octavia, and with an order that she should leave his house. Octavia obeyed. She went forth from her home, taking the children with her, and bitterly lamenting her cruel destiny.

In the mean time, while all these events had been transpiring in the East, Octavius had been making his preparations for the coming crisis, and was now advancing with a powerful fleet across the sea. He was armed with authority from the Roman Senate and people, for he had obtained from them a decree deposing Antony from his power. The charges made against him all related to misdemeanors and offenses arising out of his connection with Cleopatra. Octavius contrived to get possession of a will which Antony had written before leaving Rome, and which he had placed there in what he supposed a very sacred place of deposit. The custodians who had it in charge replied to Octavius, when he demanded it, that they would not give it to him, but if he wished to take it they would not hinder him. Octavius then took the will, and read it to the Roman Senate. It provided, among other things, that at his death, if his death should happen at Rome, his body should be sent to Alexandria to be given to Cleopatra; and it evinced in other ways a degree of subserviency and devotedness to the Egyptian queen which was considered wholly unworthy of a Roman chief magistrate. Antony was accused, too, of having plundered cities and provinces, to make presents to Cleopatra; of having sent a library of two hundred thousand volumes to her from Pergamus, to replace the one which Julius Caesar had accidentally burned; of having raised her sons, ignoble as their birth was, to high places of trust and power in the Roman government, and of having in many ways compromised the dignity of a Roman officer by his unworthy conduct in reference to her. He used, for example, when presiding at a judicial tribunal, to receive love-letters sent him from Cleopatra, and then at once turn off his attention from the proceedings going forward before him to read the letters.[1]

[Footnote 1: These letters, in accordance with the scale of expense and extravagance on which Cleopatra determined that every thing relating to herself and Antony should be done, were engraved on tablets made of onyx, or crystal, or other hard and precious stones.]

Sometimes he did this when sitting in the chair of state, giving audience to embassadors and princes. Cleopatra probably sent these letters in at such times under the influence of a wanton disposition to show her power. At one time, as Octavius said in his arguments before the Roman Senate, Antony was hearing a cause of the greatest importance, and during a time in the progress of the cause when one of the principal orators of the city was addressing him, Cleopatra came passing by, when Antony suddenly arose, and, leaving the court without any ceremony, ran out to follow her. These and a thousand similar tales exhibited Antony in so odious a light, that his friends forsook his cause, and his enemies gained a complete triumph. The decree was passed against him, and Octavius was authorized to carry it into effect; and accordingly, while Antony, with his fleet and army, was moving westward from Samos and the Aegean Sea, Octavius was coming eastward and southward down the Adriatic to meet him.

In process of time, after various maneuvers and delays, the two armaments came into the vicinity of each other at a place called Actium, which will be found upon the map on the western coast of Epirus, north of Greece. Both of the commanders had powerful fleets at sea, and both had great armies upon the land. Antony was strongest in land troops, but his fleet was inferior to that of Octavius, and he was himself inclined to remain on the land and fight the principal battle there. But Cleopatra would not consent to this. She urged him to give Octavius battle at sea. The motive which induced her to do this has been supposed to be her wish to provide a more sure way of escape in case of an unfavorable issue to the conflict. She thought that in her galleys she could make sail at once across the sea to Alexandria in case of defeat, whereas she knew not what would become of her if beaten at the head of an army on the land. The ablest counselors and chief officers in the army urged Antony very strongly not to trust himself to the sea. To all their arguments and remonstrances, however, Antony turned a deaf ear. Cleopatra must be allowed to have her way. On the morning of the battle, when the ships were drawn up in array, Cleopatra held the command of a division of fifty or sixty Egyptian vessels, which were all completely manned, and well equipped with masts and sails. She took good care to have every thing in perfect order for flight, in case flight should prove to be necessary. With these ships she took a station in reserve, and for a time remained there a quiet witness of the battle. The ships of Octavius advanced to the attack of those of Antony, and the men fought from deck to deck with spears, boarding-pikes, flaming darts, and every other destructive missile which the military art had then devised. Antony's ships had to contend against great disadvantages. They were not only outnumbered by those of Octavius, but were far surpassed by them in the efficiency with which they were manned and armed. Still, it was a very obstinate conflict. Cleopatra, however, did not wait to see how it was to be finally decided. As Antony's forces did not immediately gain the victory, she soon began to yield to her fears in respect to the result, and, finally, fell into a panic and resolved to fly. She ordered the oars to be manned and the sails to be hoisted, and then forcing her way through a portion of the fleet that was engaged in the contest, and throwing the vessels into confusion as she passed, she succeeded in getting to sea, and then pressed on, under full sail, down the coast to the southward. Antony, as soon as he perceived that she was going, abandoning every other thought, and impelled by his insane devotedness to her, hastily called up a galley of five banks of oarsmen to pull with all their force after Cleopatra's flying squadron.

Cleopatra, looking back from the deck of her vessel, saw this swift galley pressing on toward her. She raised a signal at the stern of the vessel which she was in, that Antony might know for which of the fifty flying ships he was to steer. Guided by the signal, Antony came up to the vessel, and the sailors hoisted him up the side and helped him in. Cleopatra had, however, disappeared. Overcome with shame and confusion, she did not dare, it seems, to meet the look of the wretched victim of her arts whom she had now irretrievably ruined. Antony did not seek her. He did not speak a word. He went forward to the prow of the ship, and, throwing himself down there alone, pressed his head between his hands, and seemed stunned and stupefied, and utterly overwhelmed with horror and despair.

He was, however, soon aroused from his stupor by an alarm raised on board his galley that they were pursued. He rose from his seat, seized a spear, and, on ascending to the quarter-deck, saw that there were a number of small light boats, full of men and of arms, coming up behind them, and gaining rapidly upon his galley. Antony, now free for a moment from his enchantress's sway, and acting under the impulse of his own indomitable boldness and decision, instead of urging the oarsmen to press forward more rapidly in order to make good their escape, ordered the helm to be put about, and thus, turning the galley around, he faced his pursuers, and drove his ship into the midst of them. A violent conflict ensued, the din and confusion of which was increased by the shocks and collisions between the boats and the galley. In the end, the boats were beaten off, all excepting one: that one kept still hovering near, and ng up behind them, and gaining rapidly upon his galley. Antony, now free for at Antony, and seeking eagerly an opportunity to throw it, seemed by his attitude and the expression of his countenance to be animated by some peculiarly bitter feeling of hostility and hate. Antony asked him who he was, that dared so fiercely to threaten *him*. The man replied by giving his name, and saying that he came to avenge the death of his father. It proved that he was the son of a man whom Antony had at a previous time, on some account or other, caused to be beheaded.

There followed an obstinate contest between Antony and this fierce assailant, in the end of which the latter was beaten off. The boats then, having succeeded in making some prizes from Antony's fleet, though they had failed in capturing Antony himself, gave up the pursuit and returned. Antony then went back to his place, sat down in the prow, buried his face in his hands, and sank into the same condition of hopeless distress and anguish as before.

When husband and wife are overwhelmed with misfortune and suffering, each instinctively seeks a refuge in the sympathy and support of the other. It is, however, far otherwise with such connections as that of Antony and Cleopatra. Conscience, which remains calm and quiet in prosperity and sunshine, rises up with sudden and unexpected violence as soon as the hour of calamity comes; and thus, instead of mutual comfort and help, each finds in the thoughts of the other only the means of adding the horrors of remorse to the anguish of disappointment and despair. So extreme was Antony's distress, that for three days he and Cleopatra neither saw nor spoke to each other. She was overwhelmed with confusion and chagrin, and he was in such a condition of mental excitement that she did not dare to approach him. In a word, reason seemed to have wholly lost its sway—his mind, in the alternations of his insanity, rising sometimes to fearful excitement, in paroxysms of uncontrollable rage, and then sinking again for a time into the stupor of despair.

In the mean time, the ships were passing down as rapidly as possible on the western coast of Greece. When they reached Taenarus, the southern promontory of the peninsula, it was necessary to pause and consider what was to be done. Cleopatra's women went to Antony and attempted to quiet and calm him. They brought him food. They persuaded him to see Cleopatra. A great number of merchant ships from the ports along the coast gathered around Antony's little fleet and offered their services. His cause, they said, was by no means desperate. The army on the land had not been beaten. It was not even certain that his fleet had been conquered. They endeavored thus to revive the ruined commander's sinking courage, and to urge him to make a new effort to retrieve his fortunes. But all was in vain. Antony was sunk in a hopeless despondency. Cleopatra was determined on going to Egypt, and he must go too. He distributed what treasure remained at his disposal among his immediate followers and friends, and gave them advice about the means of concealing themselves until they could make peace with Octavius. Then, giving up all as lost, he followed Cleopatra across the sea to Alexandria.

CHAPTER XII.

THE END OF CLEOPATRA.

Infatuation of Antony.—His early character—Powerful influence of Cleopatra over Antony,—Indignation at Antony's conduct.—Plans of Cleopatra.— Antony becomes a misanthrope.—His hut on the island of Pharos—Antony's reconciliation with Cleopatra.—Scenes of revelry.—Cleopatra makes a collection of poisons.—Her experiments with them.—Antony's suspicions.— Cleopatra's stratagem.—The bite of the asp.—Cleopatra's tomb.—Progress of Octavius.—Proposal of Antony.—Octavius at Pelusium.—Cleopatra's treasures.—Fears of Octavius.—He arrives at Alexandria.—The sally.—The unfaithful captain.—Disaffection of Antony's men.—Desertion of the fleet.— False rumor of Cleopatra's death.—Antony's despair.—Eros.—Antony's attempt to kill himself.—Antony taken to Cleopatra.—She refuses to open the door.—Antony taken in at the window.—Cleopatra's grief.—Death of Antony.—Cleopatra made prisoner.—Treatment of Cleopatra.—Octavius takes possession of Alexandria.—Antony's funeral.—Cleopatra's wretched condition.—Cleopatra's wounds and bruises.—She resolves to starve herself. —Threats of Octavius.—Their effect.—Octavius visits Cleopatra.—Her wretched condition.—The false inventory.—Cleopatra in a rage.—Octavius deceived.—Cleopatra's determination.—Cleopatra visits Antony's tomb.— Her composure on her return.—Cleopatra's supper.—The basket of figs.— Cleopatra's letter to Octavius.—She is found dead.—Death of Charmion.— Amazement of the by-standers.—Various conjectures as to the cause of Cleopatra's death.—Opinion of Octavius.—His triumph.

The case of Mark Antony affords one of the most extraordinary examples of the power of unlawful love to lead its deluded and infatuated victim into the very jaws of open and recognized destruction that history records. Cases similar in character occur by thousands in common life; but Antony's, though perhaps not more striking in itself than a great multitude of others have been, is the most conspicuous instance that has ever been held up to the observation of mankind.

In early life, Antony was remarkable, as we have already seen, for a certain savage ruggedness of character, and for a stern and indomitable recklessness of will, so great that it seemed impossible that any thing human should be able to tame him. He was under the control, too, of an ambition so lofty and aspiring that it appeared to know no bounds; and yet we find him taken possession of, in the very midst of his career, and in the height of his prosperity and success, by a woman, and so subdued by her arts and fascinations as to yield himself wholly to her guidance, and allow himself to be led about by her entirely at her will. She displaces whatever there might have been that was noble and generous in his heart, and substitutes therefor her own principles of malice and cruelty. She extinguishes all the fires of his ambition, originally so magnificent in its aims that the world seemed hardly large enough to afford it scope, and instead of this lofty passion, fills his soul with a love of the lowest, vilest, and most ignoble pleasures. She leads him to betray every public trust, to alienate from himself all the affections of his countrymen, to repel most cruelly the kindness and devotedness of a beautiful and faithful wife, and, finally to expel this wife and all of his own legitimate family from his house; and now, at last, she conducts him away in a most cowardly and ignoble flight from the field of his duty as a soldier—he knowing, all the time, that she is hurrying him to disgrace and destruction, and yet utterly without power to break from the control of his invisible chains.

The indignation which Antony's base abandonment of his fleet and army at the battle of Actium excited, over all that part of the empire which had been under his command, was extreme. There was not the slightest possible excuse for such a flight. His army, in which his greatest strength lay, remained unharmed, and even his fleet was not defeated. The ships continued the combat until night, notwithstanding the betrayal of their cause by their commander. They were at length, however, subdued. The army, also, being discouraged, and losing all motive for resistance, yielded too. In a very short time the whole country went over to Octavius's side.

In the mean time, Cleopatra and Antony, on their first return to Egypt, were completely beside themselves with terror. Cleopatra formed a plan for having all the treasures that she could save, and a certain number of galleys sufficient for the transportation of these treasures and a small company of friends, carried across the isthmus of Suez and launched upon the Red Sea, in order that she might escape in that direction, and find some remote hiding-place and safe retreat on the shores of Arabia or India, beyond the reach of Octavius's dreaded power. She actually commenced this undertaking, and sent one or two of her galleys across the isthmus; but the Arabs seized them as soon as they reached their place of destination, and killed or captured the men that had them in charge, so that this desperate scheme was soon abandoned. She and Antony then finally concluded to establish themselves at Alexandria, and made preparation, as well as they could, for defending themselves against Octavius there.

Antony, when the first effects of his panic subsided, began to grow mad with vexation and resentment against all mankind. He determined that he would have nothing to do with Cleopatra or with any of her friends, but went off in a fit of sullen rage, and built a hermitage in a lonely place, on the island of Pharos, where he lived for a time, cursing his folly and his wretched fate, and uttering the bitterest invectives against all who had been concerned in it. Here tidings came continually in, informing him of the defection of one after another of his armies, of the fall of his provinces in Greece and Asia Minor, and of the irresistible progress which Octavius was now making toward universal dominion. The tidings of these disasters coming incessantly upon him kept him in a continual fever of resentment and rage.

At last he became tired of his misanthropic solitude, a sort of reconciliation ensued between himself and Cleopatra, and he went back again to the city. Here he joined himself once more to Cleopatra, and, collecting together what remained of their joint resources, they plunged again into a life of dissipation and vice, with the vain attempt to drown in mirth and wine the bitter regrets and the anxious forebodings which filled their souls. They joined with them a company of revelers as abandoned as themselves, and strove very hard to disguise and conceal their cares in their forced and unnatural gayety. They could not, however, accomplish this purpose. Octavius was gradually advancing in his progress, and they knew very well that the time of his dreadful reckoning with them must soon come; nor was there any place on earth in which they could look with any hope of finding a refuge in it from his vindictive hostility.

Cleopatra, warned by dreadful presentiments of what would probably at last be her fate, amused herself in studying the nature of poisons—not theoretically, but practically—making experiments with them on wretched prisoners and captives whom she compelled to take them in order that she and Antony might see the effects which they produced. She made a collection of all the poisons which she could procure, and administered portions of them all, that she might see which were sudden and which were slow in their effects, and also learn which produced the greatest distress and suffering, and which, on the other hand, only benumbed and stupefied the faculties, and thus extinguished life with the least infliction of pain. These experiments were not confined to such vegetable and mineral poisons as could be mingled with the food or administered in a potion. Cleopatra took an equal interest in the effects of the bite of venomous serpents and reptiles. She procured specimens of all these animals, and tried them upon her prisoners, causing the men to be stung and bitten by them, and then watching the effects. These investigations were made, not directly with a view to any practical use, which she was to make of the knowledge thus acquired, but rather as an agreeable occupation, to divert her mind, and to amuse Antony and her guests. The variety in the forms and expressions which the agony of her poisoned victims assumed,— their writhings, their cries, their convulsions, and the distortions of their features when struggling with death, furnished exactly the kind and degree of excitement which she needed to occupy and amuse her mind.

[Illustration: CLEOPATRA TESTING THE POISONS UPON THE SLAVES]

Antony was not entirely at ease, however, during the progress of these terrible experiments. His foolish and childish fondness for Cleopatra was mingled with jealousy, suspicion, and distrust; and he was so afraid that Cleopatra might secretly poison him, that he would never take any food or wine without requiring that she should taste it before him. At length, one day, Cleopatra caused the petals of some flowers to be poisoned, and then had the flowers woven into the chaplet which Antony was to wear at supper. In the midst of the feast, she pulled off the leaves of the flowers from her own chaplet and put them playfully into her wine, and then proposed that Antony should do the same with his chaplet, and that they should then drink the wine, tinctured, as it would be, with the color and the perfume of the flowers. Antony entered very readily into this proposal, and when he was about to drink the wine, she arrested his hand, and told him that it was poisoned. "You see now," said she, "how vain it is for you to watch against me. If it were possible for me to live without you, how easy it would be for me to devise ways and means to kill you." Then, to prove that her words were true, she ordered one of the servants to drink Antony's wine. He did so, and died before their sight in dreadful agony.

The experiments which Cleopatra thus made on the nature and effects of poison were not, however, wholly without practical result. Cleopatra learned from them, it is said, that the bite of the asp was the easiest and least painful mode of death. The effect of the venom of that animal appeared to her to be the lulling of the sensorium into a lethargy or stupor, which soon ended in death, without the intervention of pain. This knowledge she seems to have laid up in her mind for future use.

The thoughts of Cleopatra appear, in fact, to have been much disposed, at this time, to flow in gloomy channels, for she occupied herself a great deal in building for herself a sepulchral monument in a certain sacred portion of the city. This monument had, in fact, been commenced many years ago, in accordance with a custom prevailing among Egyptian sovereigns, of expending a portion of their revenues during their life-time in building and decorating their own tombs. Cleopatra now turned her mind with new interest to her own mausoleum. She finished it, provided it with the strongest possible bolts and bars, and, in a word, seemed to be preparing it in all respects for occupation.

In the mean time, Octavius, having made himself master of all the countries which had formerly been under Antony's sway, now advanced, meeting none to oppose him, from Asia Minor into Syria, and from Syria toward Egypt. Antony and Cleopatra made one attempt, while he was thus advancing toward Alexandria, to avert the storm which was impending over them, by sending an embassage to ask for some terms of peace. Antony proposed, in this embassage, to give up every thing to his conqueror on condition that he might be permitted to retire unmolested with Cleopatra to Athens, and allowed to spend the remainder of their days there in peace; and that the kingdom of Egypt might descend to their children. Octavius replied that he could not make any terms with Antony, though he was willing to consent to any thing that was reasonable in behalf of Cleopatra. The messenger who came back from Octavius with this reply spent some time in private interviews with Cleopatra. This aroused Antony's jealousy and anger. He accordingly ordered the unfortunate messenger to be scourged and then sent back to Octavius, all lacerated with wounds, with orders to say to Octavius that if it displeased him to have one of his servants thus punished, he might revenge himself by scourging a servant of Antony's who was then, as it happened, in Octavius's power.

The news at length suddenly arrived at Alexandria that Octavius had appeared before Pelusium, and that the city had fallen into his hands. The next thing Antony and Cleopatra well knew would be, that they should see him at the gates of Alexandria. Neither Antony nor Cleopatra had any means of resisting his progress, and there was no place to which they could fly. Nothing was to be done but to await, in consternation and terror, the sure and inevitable doom which was now so near.

Cleopatra gathered together all her treasures and sent them to her tomb. These treasures consisted of great and valuable stores of gold, silver, precious stones, garments of the highest cost, and weapons, and vessels of exquisite workmanship and great value, the hereditary possessions of the Egyptian kings. She also sent to the mausoleum an immense quantity of flax, tow, torches, and other combustibles. These she stored in the lower apartments of the monument, with the desperate determination of burning herself and her treasures together rather than to fall into the hands of the Romans.

In the mean time, the army of Octavius steadily continued its march across the desert from Pelusium to Alexandria. On the way, Octavius learned, through the agents in communication with him from within the city what were the arrangements which Cleopatra had made for the destruction of her treasure whenever the danger should become imminent of its falling into his hands. He was extremely unwilling that this treasure should be lost. Besides its intrinsic value, it was an object of immense importance to him to get possession of it for the purpose of carrying it to Rome as a trophy of his triumph. He accordingly sent secret messengers to Cleopatra, endeavoring to separate her from Antony, and to infuse her mind with the profession that he felt only friendship for her, and did not mean to do her any injury, being in pursuit of Antony only. These negotiations were continued from day to day while Octavius was advancing. At last the Roman army reached Alexandria, and invested it on every side.

As soon as Octavius was established in his camp under the walls of the city, Antony planned a sally, and he executed it, in fact, with considerable energy and success. He issued suddenly from the gates, at the head of as strong a force as he could command, and attacked a body of Octavius's horsemen. He succeeded in driving these horsemen away from their position, but he was soon driven back in his turn, and compelled to retreat to the city, fighting as he fled, to beat back his pursuers. He was extremely elated at the success of this skirmish. He came to Cleopatra with a countenance full of animation and pleasure, took her in his arms and kissed her, all accoutered for battle as he was, and boasted greatly of the exploit which he had performed. He praised, too, in the highest terms, the valor of one of the officers who had gone out with him to the fight, and whom he had now brought to the palace to present to Cleopatra. Cleopatra rewarded the faithful captain's prowess with a magnificent suit of armor made of gold. Notwithstanding this reward, however, the man deserted Antony that very night, and went over to the enemy. Almost all of Antony's adherents were in the same state of mind. They would have gladly gone over to the camp of Octavius, if they could have found an opportunity to do so.

In fact, when the final battle was fought, the fate of it was decided by a grand defection in the fleet, which went over in a body to the side of Octavius. Antony was planning the operations of the day, and reconnoitering the movements of the enemy from an eminence which he occupied at the head of a body of foot soldiers—all the land forces that now remained to him—and looking off, from the eminence on which he stood, toward the harbor, he observed a movement among the galleys. They were going out to meet the ships of Octavius, which were lying at anchor not very far from them. Antony supposed that his vessels were going to attack those of the enemy, and he looked to see what exploits they would perform. They advanced toward Octavius's ships, and when they met them, Antony observed, to his utter amazement, that, instead of the furious combat that he had expected to see, the ships only exchanged friendly salutations, by the use of the customary naval signals; and then his ships, passing quietly round, took their positions in the lines of the other fleet. The two fleets had thus become merged and mingled into one.

Antony immediately decided that this was Cleopatra's treason. She had made peace with Octavius, he thought, and surrendered the fleet to him as one of the conditions of it. Antony ran through the city, crying out that he was betrayed, and in a frensy of rage sought the palace. Cleopatra fled to her tomb. She took in with her one or two attendants, and bolted and barred the doors, securing the fastenings with the heavy catches and springs that she had previously made ready. She then directed her women to call out through the door that she had killed herself within the tomb.

The tidings of her death were borne to Antony. It changed his anger to grief and despair. His mind, in fact, was now wholly lost to all balance and control, and it passed from the dominion of one stormy passion to another with the most capricious facility. He cried out with the most bitter expressions of sorrow, mourning, he said, not so much Cleopatra's death, for he should soon follow and join her, as the fact that she had proved herself so superior to him in courage at last, in having thus anticipated him in the work of self-destruction.

He was at this time in one of the chambers of the palace, whither he had fled in despair, and was standing by a fire, for the morning was cold. He had a favorite servant named Eros, whom he greatly trusted, and whom he had made to take an oath long before, that whenever it should become necessary for him to die, Eros should kill him. This Eros he now called to him, and telling him that the time was come, ordered him to take the sword and strike the blow.

Eros took the sword while Antony stood up before him. Eros turned his head aside as if wishing that his eyes should not see the deed which his hands were about to perform. Instead, however, of piercing his master with it, he plunged it into his own breast, fell down at Antony's feet, and died.

Antony gazed a moment at the shocking spectacle, and then said, "I thank thee for this, noble Eros. Thou hast set me an example. I must do for myself what thou couldst not do for me." So saying, he took the sword from his servant's hands, plunged it into his body, and staggering to a little bed that was near, fell over upon it in a swoon. He had received a mortal wound.

The pressure, however, which was produced by the position in which he lay upon the bed, stanched the wound a little, and stopped the flow of blood. Antony came presently to himself again, and then began to beg and implore those around him to take the sword and put him out of his misery. But no one would do it. He lay for a time suffering great pain, and moaning incessantly, until, at length, an officer came into the apartment and told him that the story which he had heard of Cleopatra's death was not true; that she was still alive, shut up in her monument, and that she desired to see him there. This intelligence was the source of new excitement and agitation. Antony implored the by-standers to carry him to Cleopatra, that he might see her once more before he died. They shrank from the attempt; but, after some hesitation and delay, they concluded to undertake to remove him. So, taking him in their arms, they bore him along, faint and dying, and marking their track with his blood, toward the tomb.

Cleopatra would not open the gates to let the party in. The city was all in uproar and confusion through the terror of the assault which Octavius was making upon it, and she did not know what treachery might be intended. She therefore went up to a window above, and letting down ropes and chains, she directed those below to fasten the dying body to them, that she and the two women with her might draw it up. This was done. Those who witnessed it said that it was a most piteous sight to behold,—Cleopatra and her women above exhausting their strength in drawing the wounded and bleeding sufferer up the wall, while he, when he approached the window, feebly raised his arms to them, that they might lift him in. The women had hardly strength sufficient to draw the body up. At one time it seemed that the attempt would have to be abandoned; but Cleopatra reached down from the window as far as she could to get hold of Antony's arms, and thus, by dint of great effort, they succeeded at last in taking him in. They bore him to a couch which was in the upper room from which the window opened, and laid him down, while Cleopatra wrung her hands and tore her hair, and uttered the most piercing lamentations and cries. She leaned over the dying Antony, crying out incessantly with the most piteous exclamations of grief. She bathed his face, which was covered with blood, and vainly endeavored to stanch his wound.

Antony urged her to be calm, and not to mourn his fate. He asked for some wine. They brought it to him and he drank it. He then entreated Cleopatra to save her life, if she possibly could do so, and to make some terms or other with Octavius, so as to continue to live. Very soon after this he expired.

In the mean time, Octavius had heard of the mortal wound which Antony had given himself; for one of the by-standers had seized the sword the moment that the deed was done, and had hastened to carry it to Octavius, and to announce to him the death of his enemy. Octavius immediately desired to get Cleopatra into his power. He sent a messenger, therefore, to the tomb, who attempted to open a parley there with her. Cleopatra talked with the messenger through the keyholes or crevices, but could not be induced to open the door. The messenger reported these facts to Octavius. Octavius then sent another man with the messenger, and while one was engaging the attention of Cleopatra and her women at the door below, the other obtained ladders, and succeeded in gaining admission into the window above. Cleopatra was warned of the success of this stratagem by the shrieks of her women, who saw the officer coming down the stairs. She looked around, and observing at a glance that she was betrayed, and that the officer was coming to seize her, she drew a little dagger from her robe, and was about to plunge it into her breast, when the officer grasped her arm just in time to prevent the blow. He took the dagger from her, and then examined her clothes to see that there were no other secret weapons concealed there.

The capture of the queen being reported to Octavius, he appointed an officer to take her into close custody. This officer was charged to treat her with all possible courtesy, but to keep a close and constant watch over her, and particularly to guard against allowing her any possible means or opportunity for self-destruction.

In the mean time, Octavius took formal possession of the city, marching in at the head of his troops with the most imposing pomp and parade. A chair of state, magnificently decorated, was set up for him on a high elevation in a public square; and here he sat, with circles of guards around him, while the people of the city, assembled before him in the dress of suppliants, and kneeling upon the pavement, begged his forgiveness, and implored him to spare the city. These petitions the great conqueror graciously condescended to grant.

Many of the princes and generals who had served under Antony came next to beg the body of their commander, that they might give it an honorable burial. These requests, however, Octavius would not accede to, saying that he could not take the body away from Cleopatra. He, however, gave Cleopatra leave to make such arrangements for the obsequies as she thought fit, and allowed her to appropriate such sums of money from her treasures for this purpose as she desired. Cleopatra accordingly made the necessary arrangements, and superintended the execution of them; not, however, with any degree of calmness and composure, but in a state, on the contrary, of extreme agitation and distress. In fact, she had been living now so long under the unlimited and unrestrained dominion of caprice and passion, that reason was pretty effectually dethroned, and all self-control was gone. She was now nearly forty years of age, and, though traces of her inexpressible beauty remained, her bloom was faded, and her countenance was wan with the effects of weeping, anxiety, and despair. She was, in a word, both in body and mind, only the wreck and ruin of what she once had been.

When the burial ceremonies were performed, and she found that all was over —that Antony was forever gone, and she herself hopelessly and irremediably ruined—she gave herself up to a perfect frensy of grief. She beat her breast, and scratched and tore her flesh so dreadfully, in the vain efforts which she made to kill herself, in the paroxysms of her despair, that she was soon covered with contusions and wounds, which, becoming inflamed and swelled, made her a shocking spectacle to see, and threw her into a fever. She then conceived the idea of pretending to be more sick than she was, and so refusing food and starving herself to death. She attempted to execute this design. She rejected every medical remedy that was offered her, and would not eat, and lived thus some days without food. Octavius, to whom every thing relating to his captive was minutely reported by her attendants, suspected her design. He was very unwilling that she should die, having set his heart on exhibiting her to the Roman people, on his return to the capital, in his triumphal procession. He accordingly sent her orders, requiring that she should submit to the treatment prescribed by the physician, and take her food, enforcing these his commands with a certain threat which he imagined might have some influence over her. And what threat does the reader imagine could possibly be devised to reach a mind so sunk, so desperate, so wretched as hers? Every thing seemed already lost but life, and life was only an insupportable burden. What interests, then, had she still remaining upon which a threat could take hold?

Octavius, in looking for some avenue by which he could reach her, reflected that she was a mother. Caesarion, the son of Julius Caesar, and Alexander, Cleopatra, and Ptolemy, Antony's children, were still alive. Octavius imagined that in the secret recesses of her wrecked and ruined soul there might be some lingering principle of maternal affection remaining which he could goad into life and action. He accordingly sent word to her that, if she did not yield to the physician and take her food, he would kill every one of her children.

The threat produced its effect. The crazed and frantic patient became calm.

She received her food. She submitted to the physician. Under his treatment her wounds began to heal, the fever was allayed, and at length she appeared to be gradually recovering.

When Octavius learned that Cleopatra had become composed, and seemed to be in some sense convalescent, he resolved to pay her a visit. As he entered the room where she was confined, which seems to have been still the upper chamber of her tomb, he found her lying on a low and miserable bed, in a most wretched condition, and exhibiting such a spectacle of disease and wretchedness that he was shocked at beholding her. She appeared, in fact, almost wholly bereft of reason. When Octavius came in, she suddenly leaped out of the bed, half naked as she was, and covered with bruises and wounds, and crawled miserably along to her conqueror's feet in the attitude of a suppliant. Her hair was torn from her head, her limbs were swollen and disfigured, and great bandages appeared here and there, indicating that there were still worse injuries than these concealed. From the midst of all this squalidness and misery there still beamed from her sunken eyes a great portion of their former beauty, and her voice still possessed the same inexpressible charm that had characterized it so strongly in the days of her prime. Octavius made her go back to her bed again and lie down.

Cleopatra then began to talk and excuse herself for what she had done, attributing all the blame of her conduct to Antony. Octavius, however, interrupted her, and defended Antony from her criminations, saying to her that it was not his fault so much as hers. She then suddenly changed her tone, and acknowledging her sins, piteously implored mercy. She begged Octavius to pardon and spare her, as if now she were afraid of death and dreaded it, instead of desiring it as a boon. In a word, her mind, the victim and the prey alternately of the most dissimilar and inconsistent passions, was now overcome by fear. To propitiate Octavius, she brought out a list of all her private treasures, and delivered it to him as a complete inventory of all that she had. One of her treasurers, however, named Zeleucus, who was standing by, said to Octavius that that list was not complete. Cleopatra had, he alleged, reserved several things of great value, which she had not put down upon it.

This assertion, thus suddenly exposing her duplicity, threw Cleopatra into a violent rage. She sprang from her bed and assaulted her secretary in a most furious manner. Octavius and the others who were here interposed, and compelled Cleopatra to lie down again, which she did, uttering all the time the most grievous complaints at the wretched degradation to which she was reduced, to be insulted thus by her own servant at such a time. If she had reserved any thing, she said, of her private treasures, it was only for presents to some of her faithful friends, to induce them the more zealously to intercede with Octavius in her behalf. Octavius replied by urging her to feel no concern on the subject whatever. He freely gave her, he said, all that she had reserved, and he promised in other respects to treat her in the most honorable and courteous manner.

Octavius was much pleased at the result of this interview. It was obvious, as it appeared to him, that Cleopatra had ceased to desire to die; that she now, on the contrary, wished to live, and that he should accordingly succeed in his desire of taking her with him to grace his triumph at Rome. He accordingly made his arrangements for departure, and Cleopatra was notified that in three days she was to set out, together with her children, to go into Syria. Octavius said Syria, as he did not wish to alarm Cleopatra by speaking of Rome. She, however, understood well where the journey, if once commenced, would necessarily end, and she was fully determined in her own mind that she would never go there.

She asked to be allowed to pay one parting visit to Antony's tomb. This request was granted; and she went to the tomb with a few attendants, carrying with her chaplets and garlands of flowers. At the tomb her grief broke forth anew, and was as violent as ever. She bewailed her lover's death with loud cries and lamentations, uttered while she was placing the garlands upon the tomb, and offering the oblations and incense, which were customary in those days, as expressions of grief. "These," said she, as she made the offerings, "are the last tributes of affection that I can ever pay thee, my dearest, dearest lord. I can not join thee, for I am a captive and a prisoner, and they will not let me die. They watch me every hour, and are going to bear me far away, to exhibit me to thine enemies, as a badge and trophy of their triumph over thee. Oh intercede, dearest Antony, with the gods where thou art now, since those that reign here on earth have utterly forsaken me; implore them to save me from this fate, and let me die here in my native land, and be buried by thy side in this tomb."

When Cleopatra returned to her apartment again after this melancholy ceremony, she seemed to be more composed than she had been before. She went to the bath, and then she attired herself handsomely for supper. She had ordered supper that night to be very sumptuously served. She was at liberty to make these arrangements, for the restrictions upon her movements, which had been imposed at first, were now removed, her appearance and demeanor having been for some time such as to lead Octavius to suppose that there was no longer any danger that she would attempt self-destruction. Her entertainment was arranged, therefore, according to her directions, in a manner corresponding with the customs of her court when she had been a queen. She had many attendants, and among them were two of her own women. These women were long-tried and faithful servants and friends.

While she was at supper, a man came to the door with a basket, and wished to enter. The guards asked him what he had in his basket. He opened it to let them see; and, lifting up some green leaves which were laid over the top, he showed the soldiers that the basket was filled with figs. He said that they were for Cleopatra's supper. The soldiers admired the appearance of the figs, saying that they were very fine and beautiful. The man asked the soldiers to take some of them. This they declined, but allowed the man to pass in. When the supper was ended, Cleopatra sent all of her attendants away except the two women. They remained. After a little time, one of these women came out with a letter for Octavius, which Cleopatra had written, and which she wished to have immediately delivered. One of the soldiers from the guard stationed at the gates was accordingly dispatched to carry the letter. Octavius, when it was given to him, opened the envelope at once and read the letter, which was written, as was customary in those days, on a small tablet of metal. He found that it was a brief but urgent petition from Cleopatra, written evidently in agitation and excitement, praying that he would overlook her offense, and allow her to be buried with Antony. Octavius immediately inferred that she had destroyed herself. He sent off some messengers at once, with orders to go directly to her place of confinement and ascertain the truth, intending to follow them himself immediately.

The messengers, on their arrival at the gates, found the sentinels and soldiers quietly on guard before the door, as if all were well. On entering Cleopatra's room, however, they beheld a shocking spectacle. Cleopatra was lying dead upon a couch. One of her women was upon the floor, dead too. The other, whose name was Charmian, was sitting over the body of her mistress, fondly caressing her, arranging flowers in her hair, and adorning her diadem. The messengers of Octavius, on witnessing this spectacle, were overcome with amazement, and demanded of Charmian what it could mean. "It is all right," said Charmian. "Cleopatra has acted in a manner worthy of a princess descended from so noble a line of kings." As Charmian said this, she began to sink herself, fainting, upon the bed, and almost immediately expired.

The by-standers were not only shocked at the spectacle which was thus presented before them, but they were perplexed and confounded in their attempts to discover by what means Cleopatra and her women had succeeded in effecting their design. They examined the bodies, but no marks of violence were to be discovered. They looked all around the room, but no weapons, and no indication of any means of poison, were to be found. They discovered something that appeared like the slimy track of an animal on the wall, toward a window, which they thought might have been produced by an *asp*; but the reptile itself was nowhere to be seen. They examined the body with great care, but no marks of any bite or sting were to be found, except that there were two very slight and scarcely discernible punctures on the arm, which some persons fancied might have been so caused. The means and manner of her death seemed to be involved in impenetrable mystery.

There were various rumors on the subject subsequently in circulation both at Alexandria and at Rome, though the mystery was never fully solved. Some said that there was an asp concealed among the figs which the servant man brought in in the basket; that he brought it in that manner, by a preconcerted arrangement between him and Cleopatra, and that, when she received it, she placed the creature on her arm. Others say that she had a small steel instrument like a needle, with a poisoned point, which she had kept concealed in her hair, and that she killed herself with that, without producing any visible wound. Another story was, that she had an asp in a box somewhere in her apartment, which she had reserved for this occasion, and when the time finally came, that she pricked and teased it with a golden bodkin to make it angry, and then placed it upon her flesh and received its sting. Which of these stories, if either of them, was true, could never be known. It has, however, been generally believed among mankind that Cleopatra died in some way or other by the self-inflicted sting of the asp, and paintings and sculptures without number have been made to illustrate and commemorate the scene.

This supposition in respect to the mode of her death is, in fact, confirmed by the action of Octavius himself on his return to Rome, which furnishes a strong indication of his opinion of the manner in which his captive at last eluded him. Disappointed in not being able to exhibit the queen herself in his triumphal train, he caused a golden statue representing her to be made, with an image of an asp upon the arm of it, and this sculpture he caused to be borne conspicuously before him in his grand triumphal entry into the capital, as the token and trophy of the final downfall of the unhappy Egyptian queen.